The Old Man of Kusumpur & Other Stories

The Old Man
Of
Kusumpur
&
Other Stories

Amar Mitra

Hornbill Press

ISBN-13: 9798508983710
ISBN-10: 1477123456

Cover design by: Arunava Chatterjee
Library of Congress Control Number: 2018675309
Printed in the United States of America & in India

Dedicated to
Chakori and Mainak Saha

Foreword

A writer is writing a story. If he can finish it, he feels relaxed. I have been writing for forty years or more. I do not know why I write. I had spent a long seventeen or eighteen years in the village area alone. I had nothing to do but to read good books, classical literature and write my feelings on paper with a fountain pen. I had to spend every evening writing about this and that in my camp office by the light of a lantern.

In my early age, I had to go to the remote villages as a Settlement Kanungo. My job was to record the transfer of lands, to find out and put on record the names of the sharecroppers. I discovered that my ancestors, Annada charan, Jadavcharan and Chandicharan Mitra and Ravana Soren were standing a few steps away from the Kanungo sahib. Their bare bodies covered with dust and their heads bowed down in distress. They didn't have the courage to approach me. The tribal peasants had to work always with their heads bent habitually. Maybe they were my forefathers - my great grandparents - Jadavcharans and Ravana Soren. That was the time when I began to know my India. I came to know the hunger for the land of landless, and the land-grafting of the land owners, and also family feuds for land. I thought that I would share such experiences with gram-Bharatbarsho, gaon Bharat with others. that 's why I started to write. At present, I think that I started to write with an intention to fill the black holes of my lonelynees with the sentences, paragraphs I create. I write to share my feelings with another Amar, who is my reader. I write for myself.

One must have the guts to tread the untrodden path. In this connection let me recall my experience of visiting the river Subarnarekha. I was then staying at a mufassal-gunge area eight miles from that river. During the time of "hut" (big rural bazaar two days in a week), I saw some traders and their clients crossing the river. Let me tell you that Subarnarekha is believed to have it's sands mixed with gold particles. On the other bank of the river one can see the temple of Rameswara shiva and the vast area of jungle. I did not know how to negotiate this unknown path, how to reach the unknown villagers, to get to know the people I have never met. And there were those forests, the hills and the vast fields. One morning as I was walking alone towards the river I asked some passers-by about the route I was supposed to take. The villagers were curious to know the village or the house I was going to visit. When they heard that I was going to see the river, they were visibly puzzled. Why should one take the trouble to see a river? That journey was actually my passage to the world of literature. I wished to reach the river which was both real and imaginary, the river that was accompanied by its tributaries like the river Dulong and flowed to mingle with the Bay of Bengal.

I feel that literature, like life, is a journey into the unknown, uncertain future. We write to reach to that unknown reality. While spending our days, we experience so many magical moments.

These moments had been depicted in my short stories and   novels.   I   write   for   this.

09.05.2021
Amar Mitra

Content

The old man of Kusumpur

Fakirchand of Kusumpur set out on his way to meet the Big Man. A bundle of meager belongings hung on his back from one end of a cane stick that rested on his shoulder. Old Fakirchand walked with a slight stoop. It was moments before sunrise, and the March morning was soft and cool with a genial air and earth. The cocks were still crowing. Swarms of little children were already out in the open. Old Fakirchand walked slowly, as though measuring each step, and raised both hands to his forehead in obeisance or 'pranam' to the rising sun. Yes, his eyes felt better and so did his body. In the brisk morning air he touched his rheumy eyes with his cold hands. Fakirchand was about three-times-twenty, but already the world appeared hazy to him, his limbs trembled, his skin hung loose and innumerable wrinkles crossed his face. At this age, the ripe old man felt the desire to meet the Big Man of Kanyadihi, situated on the bank of the river Subarnarekha, some twenty miles away, beyond the forest of Durgadiha. Of late he was passing through a state of mental turmoil. He decided to go and see the Big Man, whom he had never met before, for his sorrows were not one but many. His eyes, for instance, were one among them. Fakirchand knew the Big man would refer him to some quack, a wizard, the very sight of whom would heal his eyes. Of what good was it to remove a cataract, he thought: Clear it once and it comes back again! But the Big Man had many medicines, he knew of many wild herbs. Oh, it was ages since he had last seen the good earth with a clear, transparent vision. His son, too, caused him much pain. The fellow had eloped with a village wench to distant Chakulia, where he managed to get himself a job of sorts. But life at this age, without a son, was not worth living. What point was there in having given him birth if, at this fragile age, he was to be left to fend for himself, old Fakirchand brooded as he walked along. He knew the Big Man would have an answer. He expected him to find a way that would bring his son hurrying back, abandoning his woman of love. And about his plot of land, the Big Man's advice, he knew, would be providential. Fakirchand was a loner. His wife was long dead. Having to keep-his land in his possession was driving him to his wit's end. His enemies did as they pleased; they carried away every sheaf of paddy that stood on his field. Just one word from the Big Man and Fakirchand would know how to treat the rascals! And even though his wife was dead and gone, Fakirchand's sixty-year-old blood still ran warm in his veins. If only the Big man named a good girl: Even now the old man's eyes light up, his mouth waters, passion swells within him at the sight of a well-formed woman. Hence Fakirchand had braced himself for a meeting with the Big Man of Kanyadihi. The night before, he had dreamt his own death. The villagers, a bumptious lot, were hovering like a bunch of vultures, waiting for him to die. The moment he breathed his last, they swooped down, tearing at his possessions. But Fakirchand would not let that happen. He would meet the Big Man and tell him all.

Fakirchand had been hearing of the Big Man ever since he moved to Kusumpur fifteen years ago from beyond Parihati. The village was rife with tales of the big man's great deeds. All things moved, it was said, according to his wishes, everything changed according to his dictates. It was only after he moved to Kusumpur did he find a home and a patch of land. He never cared for the Big Man before, but now he did. He had never believed in those stories then, but now he felt restless. One can never tell how the mind would behave when the body grows old and infirm. Fakirchand's wife went to heaven, his son ran away with a wench, leaving him lonely to guard his own little kingdom—a thatch hut and a piece of land—like the Yaksha of the legends. Many in the village wished him dead, but he was not the person to give in easily. If only his eyes were healed, he would once more live it up with the warmth of his blood, he mused as he walked. Leaving the dusty bushes and the dry ponds of Kusumpur behind, Fakirchand found himself in a gently undulating, open, barren field of saffron gravel. The sky soared infinitely above, the moor stretched unhindered to the horizon and the light poured down from the heavens in a warm, incessant stream. In that thick light, an old, black man made his way, charting his course to a distant destination that lay beyond the moor, beyond the villages, and beyond the forests. Fakirchand's mind grew dim. He remembered with difficulty the days when he first came to this region. It was a long, long time ago. It was when an awesome flying machine of war had broken apart in the sky and came crashing down on the plains of Nischinta. Fakirchand heard a drone, like that of one of those machines of yore, approaching from afar. He turned his head and looked heavenwards, into a brilliant and dazzling sky. A helicopter, hanging on its revolving blades, flew by towards the air base of Kalaikunda. The sun changed colour, the light thinned into a brassy glare.

Fakirchand crossed the field. The day was still cool, but the sky seemed to have receded far, as he approached a narrow dirt track winding through a wilderness of tall grass and thorny shrubs. He crossed that, too, and stood before a canal in which a waist-deep water still flowed. With an advancing summer, it would be reduced to a mere trickle, but after the rains, it would again swell to a height more than that of a man and a half. There used to be a bridge across the canal. But now it had disappeared. Fakirchand looked left and right, but found no trace of it. Had he come the wrong way? No, not quite, he thought. The old banyan tree stood all right at the crossing of the Baburbani canal. The tree was there, but the bridge was gone, without a trace. Fakir studied the water with his foggy eyes and sensed a sharp current beneath. He stood helpless on the banks of the canal, which was the only source of water in a sprawling, draught-prone place. He knew there were layers of silt beneath the water and a treacherous current. He remembered old Nakphuri, who died of drowning while fishing in the canal one monsoon month and was washed five miles away to Kadamdihi. It was a hopeless case, thought Fakirchand, surveying the surrounding. His body was too infirm, his eyes too weak for him to brave a crossing. Memories of Nakphuri came repeatedly back like horrid and cautioning visions, making him sink into a stupor. And as he stood transfixed, not knowing what to do next, the day grew brighter, as the sun rose higher in the sky. It was just then that the notes of a flute wafted into his ears, bringing him back to his senses. He scanned the surroundings for the one who played so sweetly, and, before much time had passed, a black man appeared with the flute like an apparition from the void.

At long last, Fakirchand had found someone. "Where are you going, old man?" the black man asked, lowering the flute from his lips. "To meet the Big Man," Fakirchand said, taking a step forward. "The Big Man? Who on earth is he?" Haven't you heard of the Big Man? It was Fakirchand's turn to be surprised, and he let off a jeering giggle at the young man's ignorance. How was he to describe the Big Man—it was as impossible as divulging the secrets of the bird and the bee. So he broke into a song, hoping that the black man would understand the allegory. Who spreads the smell when the flowers bloom Who brings rain borne by the clouds? The flowers blossom and He makes the smell waft, The clouds gather and He makes the rain come down. The black man listened with wonder, and Fakirchand told him many, many things about the Big Man. "Are you telling the truth?" "Yes, I have no reason to lie. You don't know of my sorrows. My son has deserted me; my wife is dead. I have none one at home. My eyes don't see well. But I know the Big Man will set everything right." "Oh! Then he must be as powerful as god!" exclaimed the black man, whose skin was as lustrous as the first clouds of monsoon. "Yes, very much," Fakirchand agreed. "Then proceed," said the black man and turned to take his leave. But Fakirchand held him by the arm and stopped him from going. "How will I cross the canal" Fakirchand asked. "How do I know," the black man tried freeing himself. "Carry me across," Fakirchand pleaded with a tremulous voice. "What will you give me in return?" Fakirchand promised everything! He would tell the Big Man about him so that the black man was left without sorrows. "I'll request the Big Man to make you happy." "Really?" "Yes, of course, I am mentioning the Big Man not for nothing." With a quick, effortless jerk, the black man lifted Fakirchand on to his shoulder and went down into the canal. As he waded through the waist-deep water, the black man told Fakirchand, in bits and pieces, the tales of his woe. The black man's name was Chhotosona Mandi, whose life seemed as barren as the fields of March. He was deeply in love, with the daughter of one Bankim Hansda, and the girl loved him, too. But it had meant nothing. Hansda would not give him his daughter's hand, never. Fakirchand's body quivered with pleasure at the thought of marriage. "But why wouldn't he marry his daughter to you?" "Because I have no house, no land." "Ah, the greedy swine," thought Fakirchand with laughter building up inside him as Chhotosona Mandi stepped out of the water on to the canal's other bank. "I've helped you cross, so be sure to tell the Big Man about me," said Chhotosona Mandi., "Tell him that a youth as fresh as the clouds, loves a woman of Asanbani whose name is Bishnupriya." If only the Big Man brought them together, his sorrows would be over. He wished he could go along with Fakirchand, but his hands were tied, he had to go and work as a labourer. But he would be at the same spot the next day, waiting for Fakirchand's return. He would help him across the canal again and would expect to hear the good word. Saying this, Chhotosona Mandi let himself go in the bright sunlight and blew into the flute again, the strains of which were carried far by the wind as he disappeared out of sight on the other side of the canal. Chhotosona Mandi's affair was indeed a sad one, thought Fakirchand, and resolved to tell the Big Man everything, as he resumed his journey. The old man made a slow headway along the dry, saffron dirt track, on the one side of which was a low lying field, and a small thickly wooded hillock on the other. The day was warm. It was the last day of March. The wind was laden with the smell of Sal, Mahua and myriad flowers. Twenty years ago, he was strong as a buffalo. Some of that strength must have still lingered; otherwise, how could he come this far on a hot day? With his limpid body, hazy eyes he waddled along doggedly. Gradually, the day grew white with heat. Unfiltered sunlight struck his dark, glistening body and broke up into flares as though from sparklers. He felt his throat drying up, his face felt hard and baked, his mouth tasted bitter, and his body burnt like desert sand. The old man's eyes became dimmer still and flights of hallucination crossed his fading vision. He was in the midst of a wood and ravines. His progress slowed down.

He gasped for breath. With his tongue he sought more air and wetted his dry, parched lips. He knew it was still a long way to the big Man's house and felt intimidated. Then a strange thing happened. Old Fakrichand heard people singing. He wondered who the joyous lot were who sang when the sky rained fire. He followed the sound, and the forest soon thinned, revealing a clearing. Men and women, Santhals all of them, were gathered there, singing without a care in the world despite the oppressive heat. Fakirchand silently drew closer, his head dizzy and darkness enveloping his eyes. "What's happening here?" he asked, running out of breath. The Santhals at first took him to be some sort of a curio. "Where does it come from?” asked one man. "Will you like some rice cake?” asked another. Fakirchand felt as though his skull would crack because of the heat. He sat down in the shade of a young Neem tree.

“We are performing 'salui' puja," he heard someone say. “Give me some water to drink before I die,” mumbled Fakirchand, loud enough to be heard. Some of those who stood around called for water and others brought it in a shining pail. Fakirchand first applied some to his scalp before drinking to his heart's satisfaction. His sight came back to him and he took a long, deep breath. “Why is your puja being held here?" Fakirchand asked. Someone said something, but he was too drunk to be coherent. The women started singing again. Fakir skewed his eyes to have a look. Just then someone ordered the singing to stop. “An alien has come among us. We must speak to him. No singing now, please," the voice said. “Where are you going?” asked a veteran Santhal, who was too drunk to stop swaying. “Kanyadihi.” “Where do you come from?”

“Kusumpur." “Kusumpur to Kanyadihi — that's a long way to go!. But why are you going there anyway?" the Santhals seemed eager to know. Fakirchand felt more at ease now. He ran his eyes over the faces that crowded round. All the eyes that stared at him were bloodshot. “I am going to meet the Big Man." “Who is he, the forester, a forest ranger? "Rubbish” snubbed Fakir, surprised at their ignorance. So he told them all that he knew about the Big Man and his greatness. “Why? We don't need any Big Man; we are happy without him said one.” “Shut up," another cut him short. “We have our sorrows," he continued, "our sorrows pile up to the skies.” Old Fakirchand batted his eyelids and cast sly glances at the shapely young women. “Tell me of your sorrows and they will all be over," he said absent-mindedly. “Yes, we'll speak. Will you care for a drink?" asked one, nudging him by the hand. “How can I? I am going to see the Big Man."

"Then listen. Bad times have overtaken us. The salui festival can no longer be observed with pomp. We don't get good Sal trees any more. The forester sends them all to Kharagpur. We can no longer sacrifice a boar at the ceremonies and my daughter will, in all likelihood, run away with an outsider. We don't get timber, we don't get game to hunt .The Marang Buru is not happy with us. If we drink, police get after us and pack us off to Jhargram."

The man hid his face between his knees and cried. Those who stood around cried too. "Look, old man, you are like a god to us. Don't go away without accepting our offerings. If you don't like 'handia', have rice; if you don't like rice, have water," they pleaded. They forced Fakirchand to have rice. But he had no taste for it. He felt like puking, but it was good that his belly was full. He stood up, ready to depart. The Santhals followed him. "Tell the Big Man about us; tell him to give us back our good days," they said as they saw him off. "Be here tomorrow.

On my way back, I will have a word for you," Fakirchand assured them. The old man set out again. He had not gone much far when he squeaked with suppressed laughter, but fell pensive again. He was moved by the sadness all around. "I must carry these words of sadness to the Big Man," he said to himself. The sun had slanted already. A deep booming sound reverberated through the somnolent wilderness. Were the clouds bursting'? No, bombs were going off in Kalaikunda. A mock battle was on, ripping the silence apart. The sun was going down fast when Fakirchand neared the forest of Durgahuri. He still had the forest to cross and two villages and a field beyond that before he could reach the banks of the Subarnarekha on which Kanyadihi was situated. The Big Man lived there— tall, fair and red beneath his ivory skin. He must have greyed by now, Fakirchand tried to figure out. He had not seen the Big Man ever; whatever he knew were all based on hearsay. He recounted the things he must say to the Big man—about Chhotosona Mandi, the Santhals and about himself. There was no point in surviving like the

Yaksha—either he must have a wife or his son must come back, Fakirchand thought as he walked, without realising the sky had disappeared behind a thick foliage overhead. He was deep inside a forest. Beams of sunlight pierced through the cover of leaves here and there amidst vast pools of darkness. These forests had so much to fear in the days gone by; now they were different. Yet, there were mysteries galore. God Baram still makes his rounds of the forests silently, invisibly, riding on his favourite animals.

Beneath the towering Sal trees lie heaps of horses and elephants made of burnt clay; somewhere in the forest's elusive depths one may still run into the seat of the demon goddess, Rankini. The old man walked along the eerie path and found himself in trouble again. Three distinct tracks branched off in different directions and Fakirchand did not know which one to take. He was faced with yet another confounding predicament. Again, he stopped and looked left and right as he often did when helpless, not knowing what to do next. And, then, he noticed something move at the foot of a Sal tree. A man, was it? He wondered. "Who is it that comes this way?" Fakir called out, feeling nervous. The figure waved back at him, beckoning him near, he distinctly saw with his hazy eyes. His heart began to pound in fear. A ghost, a genie, moving like a man? Fakir asked himself. But there was nothing he could do. He was lost in the forest and had to seek help.

He moved closer and what he saw made his hair stand on end. Yes, it was a man indeed, who spoke in whispers. He looked hideous, his body dismembering from leprosy. His face appeared moist and bulbous and he lay limp on the forest floor. "Which village do you belong to?" Fakirchand asked as he threw a coin towards the ill-fated man. He did not care to touch it. Other coins lay where they had fallen. Forsaken by society, of what use was money to him? Fakirchand stood transfixed and quiet. "Death has had me," moaned the man. "Where are you going, to which village?" "Kanyadihi, to meet the Big Man." The man sat up, but said nothing. "How long has it been?" asked Fakir. "It will be five years this May." Fakirchand felt uneasy standing near him. He could not bear the sight of that horrid, disintegrating face. "Which way is Kanyadihi?" he asked the leper. The man did not answer. "If you saw the Big Man he would surely prescribe good medicines," Fakirchand said again. "Who is he?" asked the leper, this time his voice echoing in the forest. A chill ran down Fakirchands spine. He told him slowly, haltingly, all that he knew about the people of Kanyadihi. The leper listened with distended eyes and stretched forward to feel the old man, but Fakirchand stepped back, avoiding his touch. "I'll tell you the road to Kanyadihi, but promise me you will tell the Big Man about my misfortune. If I am cured, I would like to roam the village streets again," the leper said, his voice becoming increasingly heavy. He showed the Fakir the way and the old man promised the leper to return with the medicine the very next day. "If only the Big Man touched you once, your body would be healed," he repeated. Fakirchand resumed his march on the double quick. His heart was heavy. A fine youth wrecked by a terrible disease, the thought kept turning in his mind. He will tell the Big Man about him, too. Had they not helped him, Fakirchand would never have found the way to Kanyadihi, where the Big man lived. He was sure that the Big Man would provide succour to them all. The sun slanted towards the river in the west. The old man walked listlessly on, and then, suddenly, not far away, he saw the sand banks of the Subarnarekha spreading like an endless, white band across the earth. Kanyadihi must be there, the Big Man's house must be there! The exclamations involuntarily went off within him. He walked even faster now. Oh, what immense suffering people endure! he thought as he walked.

But without suffering, who would know what happiness is. It was only in search of happiness that he had come all this way, hadn't he? The evening grew sullen. Fakirchand ran out of breath with excitement. With his lean body, sagging skin and weak eyesight, he had endured much strain. He felt awfully tired. His body seemed to bend and break. If only he could rest awhile! And if in that place of rest his wife was with him and his son was by his side, his pain would have half disappeared. He would have once more sat back and stared at the world with ethereal pleasure. He would have gone and had the cataract removed, and if it reappeared, he would have gone to Kanyadihi with his son. His son would have carried him on his shoulder, or would have arranged a palanquin, if possible. The Big Man of Kanyadihi would have then healed his eyes and made the world appear sharp and clear. But that was not to be. So, at the twilight of his life, he came to meet the Big Man all alone, risking his body and soul in an arduous trek on a terrible day in March. He walked with a tremulous heart. Shadows stretched far and long. The sun went down in a pool of blackish red. Old Fakirchand felt melancholic, remembering his ruined family as the day neared its end. He at last reached the banks of the Subarnarekha. But was it Kanyadihi? Was it the place where the Big Man lived? The sullen wind had no answer; it only blew hissing past. The river had swallowed up much of the village. A few structures stood scattered, reminiscent of people's hearth. Babla trees crowded the place and wild bushes grew in abundance, and not a soul was in sight. The old man strained his eyes in the hope of seeing somebody, for he knew this was the Big Man's village. Beyond that, no village could exist; the river had taken a fearsome bend. Fatigue and hopelessness began to overcome him. His body felt limp and bloodless. Perhaps this was not Kanyadihi at all, he thought; maybe, he had come the wrong way.

Maybe, it was somewhere else, somewhere around. Gradually, darkness spread itself. The wind from across the river blew hard into the old man's face as he felt the darkness thicken around him. The footloose old villager still looked for people and he did chance to spot someone, coming his way with a lantern in hand. Fakirchand pumped all the strength into his lungs and called out at the passing man, asking him to stop for a while. "In which village does the Big Man live," Fakirchand asked. The Big Man? The stranger stood askance in the dark. With a quivering voice, Fakirchand told the man about the munificence of the Big Man, one who gives shelter to the tired, unendingly speaks of life, solves insurmountable problems with inconceivable ease, the one to whom people go seeking succour for all suffering. The stranger broke into a harsh metallic laughter. "You dream of such a man on earth, old fellow? Such men don't live anymore." The stranger shook his head and went his way, leaving Fakirchand standing alone. A pale moon rose like an ochre egg. There was nobody in the vast expanse that lay between the moon and Fakirchand, not even the Big Man; only the sand dunes and the river seemed familiar. Everything seemed shrouded in mystery. The old man's mind began to fail, everything seemed to go wrong. "You didn't wait for me, Big Man. They say people like you don't exist anymore. How will my suffering or that of Chhotosona or the leper or of the Santhals ever end, if you are not there?" Fakirchand muttered to himself. He walked down to the sand dunes where the grains of sand glittered in the faint moonlight. Standing on a sea of sand beneath a benevolent sky Fakirchand cried out in frustration and anguish, "How can I sit on guard eternally like the old Yaksha, how will I live with my hazy eyes, Big Man?" The river was there, but the man was gone. He had departed silently, leaving behind all the sorrows and sufferings and, above all, a faith in the old man's mind. "If you had to go away, why didn't you carry all human miseries with you?' The old man spoke to the river in whispers.

He perked up his ears and listened to something—the sound of feet wading through water. "Who goes, Big Man?" Fakirchand tried to dash towards the sound, but fell spreadeagled on the sand. He lay on the dune like the sky lies on the earth and all stirrings sank into a cosmic

despite the pasand in its name. No local ever gets a job here – outsiders work at the offices and courts in this town. And from the moment they arrive, they count the days to freedom from this sentence of exile. Tarapada-babu, the high school teacher, openly says that once the remaining five years of his working life are done, he'll move to Durgapur or Burnpur, buy some land, and live his life out there. What attractions do Pasandpur hold for me? We don't exactly know what attractions Pasandpur holds for people, but what we have seen is that because of the offices and courts and the narrow-gauge railway line, we are never deprived of new faces. Clerks or vagabonds, those who come never stay on. We don't see why they should. What does Pasandpur have to offer besides the unpolluted air here? The tiny toy train loses its novelty value quickly. We cannot hold back the people who come here, even if we want to. They leave. If they can't, they grow old criticising Pasandpur.

Inspector of Food Talapatra-babu and a few vagabonds are the only exceptions. Their faces are suffused with smiles as they try to pronounce the name of the town. As Talapatra-babu himself acknowledged, even those with whom he played cards in the evening paid him his bribes during the day, saying softly, here you are sir, five hundred it is. The Food Babu had never seen anything like this in his life. When he heard this, Rabilochan-babu, the headmaster of the high school, said, but this is your legitimate due, how can my nephew expect to run a business without paying you off? Examining his cards, Talapatra-babu said, not everyone understands, you know, they think all it needs is a smile to get things done. For heaven's sake, if the doctor's visit or the priest's fee or the teacher's salary isn't cleared... Talapatra-babu paused halfway, seeking his fellow players' support. The headmaster was the first to nod in assent, of course, of course... The headmaster's nephew had a kerosene oil dealership. He had been entreating the inspector to increase his quota of oil – could he not make a recommendation to headquarters? And yes, he did sell the oil on the black market at inflated prices instead of giving it to ration card-holders, but then how was he to expand his business otherwise? Talapatra-babu had found him out, and had promptly held his palm out under the table. This had taken care of the situation, but he had haggled intently first with the nephew, making off for the card session as soon as he had pocketed the payment. The headmaster's nephew's wife served tea and chanachur.

Sipping his tea, Talapatra had said, there can be no relationship between work and leisure, you know, the other thing is a matter of the day job... Of course, of course. The innocent headmaster smiled at the inspector. Thank goodness you take bribes, that's how things get done, the previous inspector had got my nephew into all kinds of trouble. He was almost arrested, saved himself only by paying off the police. Talapatra-babu didn't spend a single night outside Pasandpur during his fourteen months here. The place had offered him sanctuary, he would say, given him relief during his last days at work, so he would not leave. Why should you go, you must help my nephew establish himself first, sir. The headmaster had told the inspector deferentially, you're not exactly without friends here. Pasandpur offers sanctuary to people. Vagrants take shelter here. Besides those who are transferred on work, the rest of the visitors are all wanderers. Some on their way in, others on their way out. Some of them are empty-headed, while others are brimming with intelligence, holding on to their ponderous heads and grey matter and brain-cells carefully as they climb out of the palanquin-like bogies on the narrow-gauge railway. It's this train with two bogeys that brings people with job as well as drifters to Pasandpur from time to time. It had brought Ramshankar Talapatra too. A befuddled Talapatra-babu, halfway to old age, had got off the evening train one day with his suitcase and bedding.

His skin blackened by the smoke from the coal engine, his drooping white moustache blackened too, a faded, ancient pair of terylene trousers hanging loosely around his waist, dressed in a khaki full-sleeved sweater, his feet covered by an old, patched pair of strapped sandals, his greying hair untouched by oil for months. People had mistaken him for a vagrant who had run away from home, eyeing him suspiciously, trying to size him up – was he half-mad or entirely mad, cunning or simple, a stayer or a traveller? But when the man had said, looking around him as he got off the train, what a nice place, their suspicion had ebbed. He had not got off at Pasandpur only to declare it napasand. No one knows when Pasandpur became a pilgrimage site for eccentric vagabonds. Probably from the time the narrow-gauge railway was set up. The toylike train would frequently deposit an empty-headed or brainy drifter on the platform in the afternoon or evening and whistle its way along to the next station. There is a station here, it's true, but that's just an empty field, with neither an office nor any railway employees. There is no stationmaster, no pointsman, no tickets. There's no fixed schedule for the train either. It might not show up for two day before arriving unexpectedly one evening, whistling. It might then stay here all night, periodically snorting and emitting smoke. The headmaster cannot sleep on those nights because of the sound made by the engine's exhalations. He isn't married, living with his nephew and nephew's wife instead. One of his nephews is established, but not the other one. One of his nieces isn't married yet.

Worry has made him a light sleeper. Rabilochan-babu, the headmaster, doesn't care for the train or the engine or its bogies. Once, a rather manly drifter had got off the train and almost torn another of his nieces apart after dragging her into the jungle. Such a to-do! Pasandpur's people had decided to beat him to death. But fearing charges of murder, the headmaster had said, never mind, put him back on the train, are the people of Pasandpur really capable of killing a fellow human being? It had certainly caused a furore. The people of Pasandpur still talk about it whenever the subject comes up. What else do we have here after all besides the train and the outsiders? Even the hailstorms are not as severe as they used to me. There was a hailstorm once, a long time ago. A twenty-kilo block of ice fell into the jungle from the sky. The cowherds saw it and told everyone. Apparently the ice took seventy-two hours to melt. Just that one time. And the other time was what the terribly beautiful and rather manly vagabond had gone and done. Forcing him into the train had not proved easy, either. The guard and driver had refused, asking, where should we take him? Wherever you like, he's a criminal.

No, the man had flared up, there would be nothing beautiful in this world then. Then hand him over to the police, the railway people had said. Word would get out in that case, with his niece becoming involved, which was why the headmaster had not taken that route. He had said, the man came by your train, we're returning him. But the drifter hadn't wanted to leave, saying with a strange smile, I shall be back, no one can love the way the women here do, oh how exquisite her eyes, how bewitching her smile, how silken her breasts. There's meaning to this town. The headmaster had turned red. What meaning, he had muttered. There's a meaning to all this – why the sun here is so hot, where the winds swirl in from, why the girls here are so lovely inside. The headmaster had felt overcome. He was told that the drifter had not forced his niece into the jungle – on the contrary, it was she who had enticed him.

She was not particularly beautiful, but her eyes held the magic of water. It was the height of summer. Their joy had made flowers blossom on the palash trees in the forest. They had touched each other the way the breeze touches the flowers and the leaves. When a cowherd saw them, everyone came to know, and then the trouble started. People had raced to the spot to find the young woman with her arms around the vagabond's unclothed, rock-solid body, covering his rough chest in kisses. The sound of kisses spread through the jungle like the splashing of rain in Pasandpur. The smell of damp earth rose from the scorched clay of summer. Much more would have taken place had the cowherd not seen them. The headmaster would have had to tackle everything. The girl is now a mother of two children, living in Burnpur. She has not been to Pasandpur in a long time. Because when she visits, she has no inclination to return, forgetting her husband and family and home. Now the headmaster became Talapatra-babu's companion. No one except that drifter and this food babu had ever loved Pasandpur. Sometimes the headmaster mentioned the vagabond subtly, he had said, this spirited sunshine, balmy breeze, a woman with a beautiful heart, her eyes like a limpid pool – none of this has ever happened before, and I don't even know why they have now. Can you tell me, where is the real home of the wind that swirls about in Pasandpur? Talapatra said, oh no, my home isn't in Sonarpur, I used to live by myself there too. My home is in Midnapore, it's been such a long time since I've been there. Won't you go home? I'll stay here as long as I'm happy – after all, no one's filed a petition accusing me of taking bribes or stealing, so I'm not   likely   to   be   transferred   again.

II

One evening the headmaster Rabilochan-babu turned to Talapatra, will you do me a favour? The food inspector's experienced eye had discerned that the headmaster really was in trouble, that he really needed help. Come to my office tomorrow afternoon, he said sternly. No, this isn't for my nephew. Dropping the cards in his hand, Talapatra said, I know, I have my eye on your nephew, I know he's selling kerosene at six rupees in the open market instead of two-and-a-half as he should. Looking troubled, the headmaster responded, what can I do, he's so obsessed with money that he simply won't listen. If he listened he would be a kerosene dealer all his life. Did you know he's selling cement too? The headmaster said, he has no choice – he didn't even finish school. Do you think I enjoy listening to people saying that my nephew hasn't even passed his higher secondary exams? The other teachers taunt me. Talapatra giggled, it's all out of envy – do they have any idea that out of the twenty-six dealers in this area your nephew pays me the largest amount? The headmaster summoned his nephew's wife, can you make us another cup of tea, Lalita my dear, inspector-babu will be here for a while. No tea, said Talapatra, I'm off now Rabi-babu,we'll talk tomorrow afternoon. The headmaster wouldn't relent. He followed Talapatra, catching up with him. That's not it, I just wanted to talk about my niece's wedding. Tomorrow afternoon, then. They did talk the next afternoon. Not that Talapatra-babu took a fee for listening. But he said, pay me for matchmaking, it won't amount to a bribe. The headmaster would have to pay, for he had made a match with one of the dealers. The groom lived in Rangamati, close to Pasandpur, young, of marriageable age. Could Talapatra finalise the match, on the condition that the dowry would have to be reduced? Is that all? It'll be done. I have him under my thumb.

Talapatra-babu had said with a smile, he sells the entire rice and wheat meant for the ration-shop on the open market. Just watch what I do to him. The headmaster had told his intimate associates everything afterwards. The match would not have been finalised if Talapatra-babu hadn't butted in. The groom could not ignore the inspector. The headmaster was relieved after the marriage. Like her sister, this girl too had started frequenting the station and the jungle of palash trees. He wouldn't have been able to take it if something untoward were to happen. Talapatra-babu was a double beneficiary, extracting a fat fee for matchmaking. He would claim he needed money desperately, that there was no way to survive without money. And yet he cooked for himself, slept on a khatia, put on a freshly-washed shirt just once a week, and freshly-laundered trousers just once in two months. Someone used to visit him from Midnapore at the beginning of every month – his son, possibly. He would leave by the evening train with money. In addition, Talapatra also sent a money-order around the middle of every month. He had no bank account here. He would be anxious at the beginning of the month, looking relieved only after his son had arrived and he had handed over the money. He would keep track through the month of the ways in which his twenty-six dealers were breaking the law. Using this information, he would corner them, two hundred won't do this month, Parimal, add another hundred, I can't bear to look at what you've done with the sugar. He had got hold of a ramshackle cycle from the headmaster, promising to return it when he left. He would patrol Pasandpur, Rangamati, Shaltora, Naw-Pahari and all the other areas on this cycle. When one of the tyres was punctured, he got the headmaster's nephew to pay for a new one. The people of Pasandpur are the finest of all, he would say. One day he observed, it's amazing – when I got off the train last winter, I had so many grey hairs, and my skin sagged, but just look at the change in me over this past one year, headmaster-mashai. Really! The headmaster was astonished. Oh yes. Check for yourself.

He was right. The headmaster felt he was telling the truth. The inspector had indeed arrived with a head full of grey hair. An elderly man with a stoop who had got off the train only this past winter. Looked like a vagrant. But you wouldn't know that now when you looked at him. What hair-oil do you use, asked the headmaster. I don't use hair-oil. Then how? It's the air and the water here, I've never encountered such fresh air anywhere, not even such water, all the grime in my inner machinery has been washed away. The headmaster was pleased. As a long-time inhabitant of Pasandpur, he couldn't stand criticism. Something happened to him in his happiness, and he asked, what was that you were saying about the air? Not just the air, the sunshine too, one is warm all the time, very useful. The sunshine too! The headmaster began to mutter, do you know what this air and sunshine mean? Talapatra-babu guffawed. Meaning, what do you mean, how can they mean anything? Where do they come from? Talapatra-babu laughed uproariously again. Where on earth will it come from? What are you talking about? By the way, my days here are drawing to an end, a month and a half to go. A month and a half! And then? I'm retiring, got my letter already. Tell your nephew to increase my payment this month, all right? The headmaster asked, and after retirement? I'll go home.

A note of mourning appeared in Talapatra-babu's voice. You'll get a pension, won't you? It's a pittance. The salary's a joke, you know, my real earnings come from the dealers. The salary is just evidence of having a job. What I earn is from bribes. Can you imagine how much I have to cycle around for it? No one lets go of money easily – neither your nephew, nor anyone else. But yes, extracting bribes in Pasandpur is easy. Let's say I buy a packet of cigarettes and tell the shopkeeper that so-and-so dealer will pay, he doesn't object. My son takes away toiletries too every month, besides the money. The headmaster said, it's all thanks to the air here, don't you think? As he left, the inspector said, remind your nephew to double the payment this month... I will, nodded the headmaster.

III

Talapatra-babu arrived panting a fortnight later, didn't you tell him, master-mashai? Of course I did. The inspector had become thinner in a mere fortnight. He seemed to be combing the area on his cycle all day, returning home late at night, and becoming irregular at the card sessions. The nephew had said, inspector-babu is desperate for money, but now that he's about to retire, why should people pay him more? But he's been here so long. The nephew had chided his uncle, the headmaster, don't you speak up for him now. So the headmaster gave the inspector a seat. Let it go, it's only a matter of a few days more. Talapatra muttered, I wrote home saying I'm retiring next month – so my wife wrote back, bring money.

You have your Provident Fund, gratuity... Talapatra-babu shook his head. I've already withdrawn my Provident Fund, only the last few months' money in there now, a couple of thousand at best. And the gratuity? No knowing when I'll get it, and they'll deduct most of it anyway. I embezzled government money once for my eldest son to start his own business. The business failed, I've been ruined too – no increments for four years, they'll take away most of the gratuity, and my salary isn't high enough for a fat pension. Talapatra's hair suddenly appeared greyer to the headmaster. For the first time he realised that the inspector used dentures, for in his agitation Talapatra had forgotten to put them on. So he was looking very old, his cheeks sunken, eyes clouded over. He had aged a great deal in a fortnight. He stuttered when he tried to speak. The headmaster couldn't make any promises.

The inspector disappeared for the next few days. One evening the nephew said, the man is sniffing around like a dog, he's even invading dealers at home in the middle of the night. The headmaster said, he's in trouble, before he leaves you'd better... The nephew said, we'll give him a farewell. But what farewell? With ten days to go before his retirement, the inspector said, I'm getting an extension. Wonderful, six months more in that case, right? The headmaster inspected Talapatra closely. The man had acquired a stoop, his shoulders seemed bent. He had not shaved for at least a week, and even his eyebrows seemed to have greyed suddenly. He looked like the man who had got off the train on a winter evening. His hands shook as they picked up a cup of tea. Sipping his tea, Talapatra said, I don't need cordiality – my rates have increased, I need my payment at once. Why are you telling me all this? The headmaster seemed irked. No, not you, but please tell your nephew. The man suddenly fell silent. Then he said in a low voice, there's no place like Pasandpur, master-mashai. Nor people, and moreover, you're my friend. Yes, said the headmaster inaudibly. Then let me tell you that my wife has written, only if I hand over whatever money I have to her and my two sons will she let me enter the house. How much money do you suppose that is? I informed them, but they don't believe me. But the house is yours, what do they mean they won't let you in? No, sir, my wife is the official owner. My sons have written, if you're retiring, you won't have any money to give us – so better look for work. What do I do? The headmaster was silent, experiencing a significant lack of ability to offer advice. The next day the headmaster was told by his nephew, all lies, how can he get an extension – his corruption is legendary, the dealers in Sonarpur even beat him up, they know everything at headquarters. Never mind, he's leaving. That's why we aren't saying anything, but he's making unfair demands. If we'd known he would do this we'd also have beaten him up and thrown him out. But then how would we have done that – the previous inspector got us into deep trouble, that's why this one was spared. The headmaster said, give him a proper farewell at least, find out what he wants, a TV set if possible, probably doesn't have one at home. He doesn't want any of that, wants cash – we had thought of using the last month's payments for a grand farewell.

Pasandpur would have earned a name for itself. The inspector arrived again on the day before his retirement. Floppy trousers, khaki sweater, uncombed hair, sunken cheeks, trembling on his feet, yes I admit I lied, everyone knows there was no chance of an extension, I had tried to collect three months' extra payment in advance, but everyone's come to know, I'm a thief after all, how can I get an extension? He was raving, discovered the headmaster. When I saw how rich some of my relations were I began to take bribes in Ranaghat, then it got to be a habit. I even smuggled rice myself when I was in Murshidabad, it's all a matter of habit, during the food movement I took government-supplied rice home, all out of habit, terrible. And not just me, my family has become used to it too. When I wrote that I would go home penniless after retirement, they replied, fend for yourself in that case, you can't get away with lies... Forget it, forget the whole thing, would you like some coffee? Talapatra-babu shook his head. I took money from you too, although it was put to good use, but what do I do now, I'm in such a hole, let me see how much I can take with me, Pasandpur's air and sunshine are lovely... Talapatra-babu didn't budge even after retiring on the thirty-first of the month. Never mind the farewell, he hadn't even received his allowance for the final month. His successor had forbidden all the dealers. He's a thief, don't any of you give him any money.

Why should you have to pay if you're running a clean business? And if you must pay, give it to me, I'm the Inspector of Food at Pasandpur now. The headmaster asked, why did you have to lie? Talapatra-babu grimaced at the headmaster's question. I was forced to lie, so that I could make a little extra money. Talapatra couldn't extract any money. Nothing at all. He spent his final days wandering from one shop to another, from one godown to the next, from one house to another, returning despondently each time. Everyone promised to pay the next day, or the day after. Eventually they didn't even invite him in anymore. His days ran out. Even when they invited him in they didn't talk to him. Even when they talked to him it was just small talk, when are you going home, and so on. No one offered him a cup of tea. No farewell. People who used to genuflect before him twice a day averted their eyes now. He kept saying, make the payment, I need the money desperately, I'm retiring. No one paid any attention. Eventually he spent his days alone at a tea-shop, sitting on a bench, facing the road. Winter had left, but its last bite was still to come. A bitterly cold north wind blew every morning. It raised each of his grey hairs on end. His head drooped, his body trembled. He looked exactly like a sick, infirm tiger, its teeth fallen out, but its greed for flesh intact. He kept hailing passers-by, just a minute, Saha-babu; here, Netai; I believe you're planning to increase your wheat quota, Mandal-babu... The ration-shop owner strode past without heeding him.

Only the headmaster noticed him on his way back from school. Stopping, he said, not here, Talapatra-babu, come home with me for a cup of tea. The inspector got to his feet with a wan smile, not today, Gobindo Saha is about to return, the dealer from Shaltora, owes me three months' payment, I'm lying in wait for him. How can you, just send word, he'll send your money to you. He won't, the treacherous miser that he is. I have no choice, I can't go back empty-handed, can I. The headmaster said, the people of Pasandpur aren't traitors – all right, I shall send for him, his son goes to my school. Yes, I had always thought the people of Pasandpur wouldn't turn out this way. I'll be leaving soon, master-mashai, I'll just sit here till then to feel the sunshine and the air, why don't you go home. Ah – even breathing is such a joy here. There's meaning to this town, don't you think? The headmaster was reminded of the drifter. He had said something just like this when going far away from Pasandpur. There was a similarity. The inspector had been caught in the same web. That evening the headmaster told his nephew, all of you should give Talapatra-babu something, it doesn't feel good to see him sitting there all day. The nephew shook his head. He doesn't want a TV, he wants money, the dealers aren't interested anymore, they're all chasing the new inspector. Ask them once more. Everyone's avoiding him. They think there's no point throwing money at him now that he's retired – he took quite a lot during these twelve months, after all. The headmaster couldn't accept this. He realised that his nephew was also avoiding Talapatra. But there were other people in Pasandpur.

When they heard, they said, this can't go on, the man just sits there breathing in the dirt and grime, he's aged visibly, we can't bear to see this. No one in Pasandpur can be allowed to be unhappy. Those of us who were long-time residents of Pasandpur said, how much does he want, we'll take up a collection, let him go back home. Talapatra shook his head at this, no, the dealers must pay, why should you, I didn't do anything for you. That doesn't matter, you've lived in Pasandpur for over a year, we shall give you a farewell so that you can go back home. Talapatra-babu kept shaking his head, mumbling, whom will I go back to? They know money, but they don't know me. I made a big mistake, if I had come to Pasandpur earlier, thirty-five years ago, I wouldn't have developed this habit of taking bribes. The air and sunlight here mean something, don't you think, that's why I cut down on the bribes here, I used to earn a lot more at Sonarpur... Talapatra-babu kept repeating the same thing for several days, there on the roadside. The man began to change visibly. If he had come here thirty-five years earlier, he might have never taken bribes, he rued. The bribes had done him no good. He had just become slaves to his wife, sons, and money. Ah! What a lovely place Pasandpur is, even my grey hairs had turned black. Then Inspector Talapatra disappeared suddenly. That is to say, he boarded the train without being observed by anyone. The next day we confronted the guard and the driver, have you taken the inspector back? The aged driver, covered in coal-dust, and the aged guard both began to chortle, yes we took him back, the last time all of you had forced a vagabond on us, this time we took him back of our own volition, get in, Talapatra, we told him, why spend any more time here? He got in? He did, but he has promised to return, he won't abandon this place – just as it is easy to take bribes here, it's also possible to live here happily without taking bribes, here grey hair turns black, teeth stop wobbling and set themselves firmly back in the gums, sagging skin turns taut, eyesight improves, apparently there's meaning to living here, there's... The guard and the driver, two aged men, chattered on. The headmaster's eyes misted over. Talapatra won't return. A month and a half later, Ramshankar Talapatra's sons came instead, two demons in search of their ungrateful father. They began to scream, the swine has escaped. Where does he think he can hide, we'll find him and get our money. The people of Pasandpur beat them up and forced them back into the train. Boarding, they said they would take revenge on their father, or on Pasandpur, Sonarpur was much better, even though their father had been beaten up there he had made lots more money, Pasandpur had corrupted him. Now the headmaster of Pasandpur gazes at the railway lines all day long. He has retired, after all. The lines are visible clearly from his veranda. I wonder what he stares at. Even though he cannot recognise people a couple of feet away, now and them he calls out to his nephew's wife, isn't that a drifter there, bent over and covered in coaldust? Could it be Talapatra-babu? Or is it the beautiful man who had come earlier... Inspector-babu.... he-e-e-e-re... The dust blows across the empty road. The summer winds are encroaching on Pasandpur, a little at a time. The nephew's wife's eyes mist over too. She covers her mouth with the end   of   her   sari.

(Translated from the Bengali by Arunava Sinha)

Marcopolo Travels: 2020

The epidemic invaded one city after another, in silence, unnoticed. When they realized, the cities began to close down. The term was "lockdown." Before it was declared, and as it rolled on, people became homebound to their countries, cities, and villages. One of them had started for Venice, Italy. Marco Polo, the wanderer, on his way back to Venice, had arrived in a new country. So began this world-travelogue. Lockdown is underway in Venice, Italy.

A video came out about a month ago at 2:30 p.m. Not a single person around. Only the quiet movements of a few pigeons in a silent city. Church bells. Marco Polo, a man from Venice, a traveler of the world, is passing through many a country, many a town to find his homeland. Mister Mayor, listen to him, about the cities and those settlements that he has crossed. Alas my friend! There remain no people in those cities now. Exhaust fumes from factory chimneys have been comatose for more than a month. Wanderer, carrier of this news, Marco Polo, faces the Mayor of Cezan. The city sits on the banks of the river Cezan after which it was named. Cezan means beautiful.

For the beauty of this city is unparalleled. "Mr. Mayor, I have reached Cezan after so many towns and settlements. From across the river, I looked at the city, so splendid! The shrines, those impeccable minarets and the extravaganza of those theatres!" Marco doesn't know how he arrived here. He only walked this earth. Listen my respected Sir, I don't know which Marco Polo is this person. The man from 750 years ago, or later? As a child, I suffered from malaria, typhoid, and jaundice. At the wake of that springtime ailment, Vidyadhar cowered under the mosquito net at home, and I scribbled in pencil, calling it news. Those were my first writings. First ever attempt at the craft... I would draw a plane and report the news under it— 'So many people have died in a plane crash.' Yes, that was the time a Pan American airplane, about to land in Dumdum, crashed in Kaikhali. There were heavy casualties. After so many years, here I am, still writing, reporting records of the pandemic. Attend, honorable Mayor, the foreboding for death is anything but new.

Japan overcame Hiroshima-Nagasaki; Eastern Europe survived Chernobyl, the plague, the Spanish flu, the French flu. How many have died in epidemics? Scared of the deadly virus, I have crawled under the net. I shall report what I see. This unseeable assassin flies from one continent to the other killing people. As a child, I had heard of such invisible flights of Ma Shitala at the onset of spring. When Shimul and the butea come abloom, silk cotton bursts in the air, deep redolence of the mango blossoms saturate the sky and the monks of Gajan bellow, "Let's all surrender at the feet of Mahadev!" They roam about the village roads and with them the deities of cholera and jaundice too join in their teams looking for humans. The dogs can smell the sinister Gods and, tucking their tails between their hind legs, they slip inside the bushes and pant, exhausted. What do I do now? I am writing the news sitting under a mosquito net. Reuters, P.T.I. Associated Press (AP), private correspondent. The way they send out news to the outside world, I shall do the same. I, the old hag of a messenger, shall report about the invisible killer. Flying on a witch's broom it reached the metropolis. From the metropolis, it rode on a donkey to the suburbs. From the highways of Tehatta,

Chandannagar, Siliguri, New York, Venice, Sydney, and Delhi, to the cramped alleys. Let me come back to Marco's words. The Mayor of Cezan and Marco faced each other. Marco was talking about the lockdown. Kolkata, Patna, Delhi, Lahore, Kabul, Samarkand, the city of Nur Sultan, Astana, Moscow... all asleep. There were no people on the streets. Wild animals prowled. An invisible virus had taken over the world. So, what you are saying is that the governor and the Mayor have ordered everyone to go home by declaring a lockdown. But then, how will the people survive if they go back home – who will till the lands and build the palaces? "No one," Marco said. "Production stops?" asked the Mayor of Seychelles. "Yes, mills and farms, all retired." "The markets, entertainment centers?" asked the Mayor. "None remain." "Theaters, operas?" "All closed." The Mayor shuddered, "What a terrible thing you report, Marco Polo." "Everyone has gone back home, or they are heading there. Hundreds of frightened and hungry people are walking hundreds of miles on their way home," said Marco Polo. As he spoke, Marco looked out the window and saw the city on the other side of the river, as if her beauty had somehow changed. How handsome are the men and women of this wonderful city! The colorful frills of their gowns, the fine cloth on their heads, nose rings, exquisite beads around their necks, red-green-blue rings on their fingers – Marco saw them as he crossed the river. How long have you not heard the chatter of people? The relaxed footsteps of humans, songs, roasted meat, bread? Beautiful girls like colorful butterflies? Musical instruments, musicians, dombra, garmon, flute – all are in this city. This was the first time the mayor of Cezan saw Marco. Globe trotter Marco Polo came to the Tatar somewhere on this continent 700 years ago. This person here, too, was Marco Polo. Did he walk 700 years back, or did he emerge with the legacy of his ancestors? The Mayor noticed Marco's skin was sunburnt, his golden hair awash in gray. This man resembles the pictures of Marco that the Mayor has seen. Of course, it depends on what you would consider as semblance. The Mayor found similarities in the shape of his chin and eyes. That pointy chin, blue irises, and a face that looked cleansed with water. A beard grows on his face due to the lack of regular shaving. The Mayor himself was six and a half feet tall, robust . He was middle-aged. The Mayor knew things. A foreigner had come to the city. They said that he had arrived hundreds of years back, from the city of Venice, from the far West. It seemed to the Mayor that the man was wearing the dust of numerous villages, the winds of many countries, the memories and dreams of many years. The man said that he'd almost forgotten about this town as he traveled. He loved to travel. One day as he was walking around, he suddenly saw that there was no one in the yard, nobody on the road. Horses had bridles on their muzzles but no saddles on their backs. Bridles meant that they were not wild but domesticated and pets.

They had masters. But now, they wandered alone looking for food. The masters have gone indoors and abandoned them. The Mayor was astonished. He said, "I have never heard of such a thing. This has never happened in this city. There are no abandoned horses, dogs, or cows in this city – our cattle are kept at home." "Your Excellency, Mayor, the lord of our city, it has, indeed happened elsewhere. On my way to the city of Venice, I went the wrong way in the whirling wind. Then changed my route again to somehow reach the city of Cezan." The Mayor looked at Marco Polo. His eyes showed signs of fear. Marco said, "Sir, I have been to many a town in my long journey and people are afraid of looking at other people's faces." "Marco Polo, Venetian wanderer, please relate what you have seen, I welcome thee," the Mayor implored. Marco said, "Then, let us listen to the messenger." "Who is the messenger?" the Mayor asked. "I have been a foreigner, a foreigner in all countries. May be even in my own hometown, Venice, if I go there now.

When I returned to Venice with my father and uncle in 1229 after 25 years, everyone took us as foreigners and refused to call us as their own. My relatives too. We had to prove so many things. That's a story you better keep for another time, Honorable Mayor." "I asked, who was the messenger?" The Mayor prodded with the same question. "Honorable Sir, he is the one who tells Marco everything.

You don't need to concern yourself about how he does that. To keep sources secret is the way of the trade." The Mayor seemed satisfied with Marco's reply. "Proceed, then." Messenger's report: I had stopped interacting with others for fear of the Coronavirus as of 14th March. The 15th and 16th March, the next two days, I sat at home. But Kolkata was Kolkata. Hordes of people on the buses and trams. I didn't see anything alarming on television. Only a fleeting warning on the arrival of an invisible assassin in the city. 16th March was sunny. Arindam Bose called at 9 a.m. to tell me the news of Subrata Mukherjee's death. Subrata's death got me out of the house again. I walked to the Metro station under a ruthless sun. The metro was relatively empty, but I still had to brush past people. I had my mask on. It felt uncomfortable. I took an auto-rickshaw to Sonarpur. We were yet to cross the Garia bridge when I saw a huge crowd by the side of the road. A long queue of people – their faces hovering over the shoulders of others. The women had brought offerings for the goddess – coconuts, confectioneries. The goddess must be Shitala or Kali. Brass bells rang. Why was it like that? There was no fear. I could see from the auto-rickshaw that nothing was different. Shops were open, trading was going on as usual. People strolled, swinging shopping-bags in their hands. I could hear the relentless honking of cars. Young civic police clad in green and blue attempted to control traffic with their batons. Cloth masks covered their faces. People crossed the roads; vagrants went on standing in the middle of the road unable to decide which way to go. I was going to meet a dead friend.

Subrata of Barrackpore had passed away at the Liver Foundation Hospital in Sonarpur at 11:55 last night. He was calling me, "Come, my friend, come see me." On my way to Sonarpur, I noticed that the greenery from years ago had disappeared. It was concrete upon concrete. So many floors, apartments, stacked on top of each other... so many people in such a small place.

2

After you reach Sonarpur, you must get into a different auto-rickshaw to get to the Liver Foundation Hospital. At Sonarpur, autos and buses were running, rickshaws screeched, rabbles of people of all ages busied themselves with an endless number of occupations. I walked in the acid sun. The auto stand was not very close to the railway. I could move fast with people on the street. No one seemed to know anything, no one cared who the invisible killer had taken hostage. Sonarpur had changed.

I remembered, many years ago on a rainy afternoon, I was driving to Kolkata via Sonarpur. It was raining a lot and the car stopped suddenly. Some fish crawled peacefully on the wet road. Sonarpur with its uncultivated fields and swamps overgrown with Hogla reeds, was no more. Everything had been erased. I crossed the railway line, walked some distance again. It was almost 11:30 when I finally arrived. It was very difficult to look at Subrata. The face of my handsome friend had blackened, as if the dusts of an entire kingdom had settled on his face. As was the case with Sonarpur. Sand filled the hot air. But amidst all that dust, there was this butterfly – a little away from where Subrata lay in the shade. How the colors played on its wings! It perched on a wildflower and sipped honey. The world was as it has always been. For a few seconds, the colorful butterfly fluttered over the ever-sleeping Subrata. It seemed his eyes opened to meet hers. Then there was no butterfly. Subrata shut his eyes again. On hearing this, the Mayor said, "I didn't see anything unusual in this description. That butterfly is not in the city of Cezan. I can't say why, but there used to be so many.

Did it die?" The Mayor sounded concerned. Marco said, "No, she flew away. There must be butterflies in the forests of your city. I am sure of it. But the one that fluttered about his friend was not common. Of course, there are butterflies in the city of Cezan. It is a big city. If they have gone away, they will return. Cezan seems wonted. But the world is not, at least from what you say." The Mayor's voice returned to normal. "In the context of the current state of the world, the situation in the city of Cezan, is unusual. Life here is unusual," Marco said. The Mayor said, "It is true that those quiet solitary cities and villages are where all animals and insects now roam free. So, maybe we don't have the butterflies here in Cezan – they have flown to other peaceful kingdoms." Marco thought silently about that butterfly – how many colors fluttered on its wings! Returning to the previous context, the Mayor said, "A friend goes to visit another who has passed away; a town runs as usual; butterflies feast on floral nectars.

They sound normal. I also heard that once on a rainy day, some fish crossed from one side of the road to the other. How big were the fish?" Marco had heard it from the conversation of the three passengers sitting inside the auto rickshaw. He heard that the fish were called Koi. The Mayor said, "You didn't ask if the fish that walked on the street on a rainy day had two legs, or whether they stood up vertically on their tails, checked their surroundings, and then moved on. Or maybe, they walked on their fins. I've heard such fish could once be found in Africa. At some point they stopped mutating. Otherwise, they would probably be humans by now." "I also heard that or probably read it in a story. But the fact is, it is not like that anymore. The water bodies have been filled and mansions have been erected. Those fish may have become extinct, or their normal production may have ended. People gave birth to them, and then they ate them." "Which way did the fish go, from the east to the west?" Marco said, "Maybe to the east. Now the East is closed by a huge wall and barbed wire." The Mayor looked over the windowsill. It had started snowing. Winter was waning and spring was on its way, but there was no end to snow. This time the winter has been long. The Mayor was wondering if this traveler knew how to play chess. He began to arrange his army. Marco was thinking about the fish; the story could very well be a rumor... So many truths and lies float about in the cities these days. If fish walks ashore, it could be a merman or a mermaid whom no one has ever seen, including Marco. So, that is the end of the problem. But were they moving out of one body of water to another, or were they evolving for good? Do they no longer need water, air, light, or darkness to survive? The creatures of darkness would become stronger than ever without the support of any of the elements. Marco was startled. The virus, COVID-19, is constantly mutating. He heard it on the way. Is the COVID-19 like that? The messenger says: Homebound since the 18th – like so many others. The television relentlessly asks people not to gather. Everyone MUST stay home. A video from Venice, Italy, arrived at the crack of dawn on WhatsApp. Silent noon. Not a person around. Which city is this? The camera moves through the quiet alleys along the banks of the canal. The boats are tied up without owners or customers in sight. Shutters on all shops are drawn down. No sign of life on the road. It seems like the winner murderer Coronavirus is showing me the carcass of a city: 'See what I have done to the people!' Alleys that feel so much like our Kolkata. And that canal! Speed boats, gondolas caught in a strange torpor, the shadows of the magnificent architectural edifices lie fallen on the somnambulant water. The country of the ancient Renaissance is asleep with its massive mansions. As I mentioned at the outset, Marco Polo was born here and started his journey from here. Marco remembers the young man's desire to see the city. He was tired of wandering in the woods. Then one day, we arrived in a town called Isadora, the city where perfect telescopes and violins are made. When one's mind is conflicted about choosing one of the two beauties, one finds a third here, which is even prettier. The young man had imagined such a city and he had walked all his life to get there. But when he arrived, he was old. Sitting somewhere in the center of the city, he was looking at the young people. He saw a city that looked uninhabited. Old monuments, pigeons, eagles and kites... This is how the video of Venice looked to me. Antonio Vivaldi, the great music composer was born in Venice. He holds a high place in the history of symphonic and operative music. The music in Venice has stopped.

The video reaches a spacious attic. It seems like it used to be a place of joy. The church bells of the final hour is ringing. Pigeons peck on grains on the ground. There are pigeons now. I understand what Venice has become. Everyone has crept back into the houses to survive. This is how we have to evacuate the city. In this way we must leave the whole city to the pigeons and hide inside our homes. The Mayor said, "Are you here on your way back to Venice, Marco Polo? I had never dreamt that you would come to the city of Cezan. 700 years is not a short time!" Marco said, "I don't know where I'm returning to, sir, but I'm coming back. And on my way, contradictions galore. Look in the mirror, what was there is not anymore. The mountain used to be on the west where a desolate steppe now prevails. It doesn't end at the horizon. I don't know where or how long it goes on." "Nikolai Ivanovich would know," the Mayor said as he shuffled chess pieces. Marco looked at the Mayor's face in surprise. The Mayor said, "A mathematician, but he is no more. If you go to Cezan University, many mathematicians there would be able to measure this distance." "Where is he?" "That will also be clear there," the Mayor said. Marco said, "There is no limit to infinity. Oh, Mayor, the more I measure, the farther it moves. Go as far as it can, mathematicians can't resolve it.

Sir, I have come from the city of Kolkata – infinite is the distance. Everyone is leaving the city. So did I." Listening to this, the Mayor of Cezan asked, "Why is everyone leaving?" They are returning home. The invisible killer roams around, and all the shops, factories have shut down in fear. Crops are withering in the fields; vehicles are paralyzed on the sides of highways. Due to the restrictions on movement, there are no passengers. The driver and his assistant are also returning home on foot." "Your words are steeped in sadness," said the Mayor. If you tell me how the city is, I will feel a little relieved. You describe things perfectly. I have not seen that city. One man cannot see all the cities and ports in one lifetime, so we have to hear about them from others." "I'm cold, in need of Vodka," said Marco. The Mayor was quick to make arrangements. His attendant served liquor and well-cooked veal with fruit, grapes, pistachios, nuts and graham, green lettuce, and mulberry. Marco was happy. He relaxed. How many times could he go on a trip if he had this supply of food and drinks? He could travel around the country to witness cities and towns. His body warmed up, his hunger too was satiated for now, at least. He carried stories of hunger.

Cities and settlements do not necessarily mean mansions, highways, automobiles, phaetons, and airplanes. They do not mean theaters, foods, and drinks overflowing with merriment, playgrounds, and bars. The city had revealed to him a destitute mother, and hapless people huddled inside drainpipes, and slums – seven people crammed in a room. Marco came to know people who gasped for air for they didn't have enough breath. His inebriated head swam mildly. He began to explain the map of Kolkata to the Mayor. A river to the west. The city stops at the banks of that river. And the green pasture in the heart of the city where one went to see the sun set. The west of this city is not west of any location. The west can be viewed from many places. But from all the places in the west, the holy river Ganga could be seen. There was no west on this side of the river. Another town sits on the other side. From there the west stretches on to infinity, beyond the eternal longitude. Once, Marco stood in that wilderness at the heart of the city and watched the sun set behind a castle. In front of him, a vagrant mother, too, looked on with her child on her lap. Marco said that he had seen the sunset from various places in Kolkata, but the sun god, going down in a circle of blood in front of a beggar mother who showed it to her daughter – that, he had never seen. The mother said that the city used to be hers, but it no longer is. The child was conceived hoping that it would return to her. Then, many people in the city, obese and frail, heads held high and low, people tall and short, all of them, they started walking towards the sunset through that green desert... "Why towards the sunset?" the Mayor asked. You must go somewhere. O Mayor, some people walk to the west, some go to the east, where, the sun will rise the next day. The woman went in the other direction. "Did the horizon flow in that direction too, like the steppe?" the Mayor asked. "No," Marco said after a while. The multi-storied buildings lined up like a wall. But it seemed as if the young beggar-mother went through it.

Nothing could stop her. I followed her but got lost. The news was circulating. People were afraid to touch the newspaper. They listened to what they heard. No one could tell truth from lies and rumors anymore. The epidemic was entering from the airports to the towns. People went home for the fear of it. The Mayor said, "there is no epidemic in Cezan. Marco, you are welcome in this city. You tell me what is happening in that other city, what is happening in those countries." "Listen, Mayor ..." And Marco Polo's world tour began.

(Translated from the Bengali by Bishnupriya Chowdhuri; Published in 'The Antonym', April'21)

The poet lives in a village by the Haldi river

They were farmers by trade. The poet's father tilled the land. His uncle too. The poet said they've been farmers for seven generations. There was a time when no ledger existed; no one parceled off plots; nothing like a land-office had emerged; and none had heard of a collector whose job was to extract rent. Only land lived. Land for all. People in the village shared it according to their needs. After all, how much does one need? The rest remained intact – no one even glanced at it. An admirer of the poet, the young bard Selim Malik, arrived from the ancient port of Tamralipta and asked, "So, what happened to the rest of the land?" "Didn't I just say it stayed untouched?" "But then, wouldn't it turn into a jungle!" The poet said, "It did. Birds came to nest. Well, we have to make space for the birds, don't we! We can't burn the trees, nor can we chop them down – we have to preserve everyone." "Birds perch on branches, fly in the sky – what dwelled on the ground?" "Why, deer, earthworms, frogs, snakes, reed cats, small tigers, hurals, butterflies, fireflies, and more..." "Have you seen them?" The poet replied, "Haven't I! Once on a moonlit night, two deer strolled onto our yard." "And then?" "They asked, 'Where can we get some water, sir?'" "And then?" "I enquired, 'Don't you have any water-chestnut plants in the forest?' "The deer and his mate burst out laughing – they rolled on each other in mirth. 'Oh, Sukumar Ray – we read it in Kishalay.' They stopped for a breath and said, 'It hasn't rained for a while – we came in search of water.'" "Did you give them water?"

"Yeah, I did – in a large bowl. They quenched their thirst, and right then, the clouds rumbled." Selim probed, "Did it rain?" "They weren't really a deer couple. They were the god and goddess of the rainclouds." Selim prodded again, "But you said they were deer!" "Did I? My mistake. They were black in color, like rain filled clouds. They drank the water and disappeared into the deepening gloom. "Then the clouds yowled – a howl like a pregnant cow ready to give birth. Hear me, Selim, when you offer a drink to the thirsty, skies fill with clouds. When you feed the birds breadcrumbs and biscuits, clouds float onto the sky and the earth yields plenty. If you see butterflies flitting from flower to flower, feasting on the nectars, let them flutter about. Know that rains have finally come after two years of drought in the distant lands of Somalia in Africa – famine has ended there." This is The Poet. He lives in a hut. Inside, a crude bamboo shelf holds his books. He rests on a cot of rope. A ragged quilt is his bedding and another, folded at the foot of the bed, covers him in winter and monsoon nights. He has a mat that he spreads outside to sit and write his poems on a small desk. He writes sometimes with pencil or a fountain or ball-point pen. Young poets gather and take the poems away.

The poet travels with them to Kolkata, to the Poetry Conference in Haldia – there he listens to poems. But he doesn't read his own poetry. He wanders about, as is his wish. At times, he goes to the river. He tells the boatmen that he owns an island in the ocean. A youthful boatman asks, "In which ocean?" "Why, the east sea, of course." "Where is the East Sea?" "'The breeze drifts in from the east sea.' Both Rabi Thakur and Kalidas have mentioned the East Sea. The ocean here was once known as the East Sea – but that is neither here nor there. If you travel eight hours by day, rest for half an hour on the shores, and sail eight more hours by night, you will reach a large bay – Gurguri isle is right there." "Gurguri island – what's that like? Never heard of such an island!" The young boatman queries his grandfather. The old boatman states casually, "There may've been a Gurguri island once – but not anymore." The poet overhears the comment and protests, "What do you mean 'not anymore?' It was there last night, but not today?" Nope, not there. The old boatman, who's at the end quarter of his lifespan, shakes his head. No longer can he hold the rudder straight or row vigorously, but his place is in the larger boat. His eyes are still sharp, and he can still fathom correctly. He is the compass. He can tell directions by checking the ocean currents, flow of the wind, and the stars above. He knows which breeze travels toward the temple of Jagannath and which one heads toward the ashram of the sage Kapil. Only this wizened grandfather can gauge the tides and tell when to shout out the name of Badar Pir and raise the anchors of the boats. He knows of islands that aren't inhabited by people, only birds, trees and plants, snakes, frogs, and insects. He knows, there was an island named Gurguri, but no longer. The man said Gurguri. Says it's his island – so, it must be somewhere! The poet says he hears from the island every single day. The Gurguri birds flew in with some vital news even last night: there's been an abundant harvest of chilis and grapes this year. The Gurguri birds feed on grapes and the parrots eat chilis. "That island is no longer there," said the old boatman. The poet smiled, "It must have gone off gallivanting somewhere, but it'll return." The young boatman questioned, "Does an island roam on its own?" The island of the Gurguri birds does.

Being at one place is boring. The young one asked, "What's the bird like?" "Sooo big!" The poet stretched his arms wide. "You may say each one is huge like a duck." The old man shook his head, "Not at all. They are teeny weeny birds – smaller than a sparrow." "Maybe. I just spoke about a duck." The poet talks about the island to another young admirer, poet Avijit of Kolkata. Avijit has translated his poems into English and the book's been published in England. The poet says, once he drifted on his Gurguri isle and reached England. In England he visited Buckingham Palace, Queen Victoria's grand-mothers, the rivers Thames and Avon, but he couldn't meet with Shakespeare, who had survived one epidemic and then, died. That was 400 years ago! The poet said, that may be true. But the fact of the matter is that he hadn't been able to meet with Shakespeare. How could it possibly have happened? For he wasn't alive! "Suppose you come to see me after 400 years. Can you? I'd be long gone and transformed into a Gurguri bird – floating atop the ocean waves. My island moves – you won't be able to trace it." The young poet Avijit said, "Why not come to Kolkata with me." "Yes, I'll go. I'll visit Lalbazar[i]. They snatched away one of my notebooks. I'll go to take it back."

The poet was beaten black and blue in Lalbazar. They gave him the third degree: "Is this straight or round?" The poet had replied, "Like an orange." They hit him with a cosh. "Which direction does the sun rise?" "In Gurguri island." "No, in the United States." The poet thought, 'The synonym for 'police' is 'foolish'.' "Where is Harilal Ray?" "In the Bay of Bengal, in Gurguri island." "Where is that?" The poet said, "Within and without the ocean." Harilal was a traitor. The poet was the writer and publisher of his magazine. He had torn down the state system with his poetry. How did he do that? He had written, "My country doesn't represent me... la... la... la... la..., pik... pik... pik..., jhim... jhim... jhim... jhim...!" "What do these words mean?" The words had slipped out of the poet's lips, "The Gurguri bird knows." The Gurguri bird was birthed right then and there – in that cell of violence. The poet was soundly thrashed, but he didn't reveal anything. He only said, "Harilal might be in Gurguri island." And the island was born at that moment, in that Lalbazar cell of whippings. He had almost whispered aloud, "Harilal lives beyond the seven seas and thirteen rivers now – in New

York City, in the coast of the Atlantic Ocean." The poet knew Harilal had glided far by riding on his Gurguri island. After he had disembarked, the island drifted again through the Hudson river into the ocean. Otherwise, the American police would've arrested it. American police are nasty. Naturally, law enforcement in every nation is vile. They visibly strangle people dead on the streets; they pick up people from their homes and hide their dead bodies.

American police would have slaughtered the Gurguri birds, fried them in butter, and consumed them. The young bard Selim asked, "Do you remember Lilabati-di[ii]?" "She lives in a faraway island. We exchange poems." Lilabati is a poet. The poet had fallen in love with her. Lilabati respected him. When the poet had gone underground, she had secreted him in her home for a while. During that time, Lilabati and her husband had taken good care of him. The poet would write his poems and go to sleep. Then Lilabati came in to take the poems away with her. In exchange, she left her own verses near his head. For as long as he resided there, this was how they swapped poetry. The poet's creations were published under Lilabati's name and hers were printed in his. Many moons later, at the end of the emergency period[iii] and the Lalbazar episode, the poet claimed Lilabati still sent her poetry to him. But she didn't take his. Actually, Lilabati had moved abroad with her physician spouse. In that foreign land, she stopped writing poetry. But the poet claimed that his poems were hers. No one could question his veracity. Whatever he said was the truth. As Ram had emerged in the bard's imagination, so had the epic. The poet didn't write about Lilabati, but himself – Rim rim rim – your poet is in a faraway land In farms, hills, trees, and amid sea-sand Wafting fragrance of a guava flower Poet, your touch has so much power r r r r r... R r r r r r R r r r r r The poet argued that since Lilabati had written about him, the poems should be published under her name. And everything written about Lilabati saw the light of day under his name. Lilabati's poems were about birds, trees and butterflies. They were about the land, the breeze, the clouds, and about the rain and sunshine. When the sky drooped low and the clouds darted casting shadows that chased them, the dark poet ran after, "Please stop... stop please..." "You ran?" "No, not me. My grandfather, Poet Purnachandra." "Was he a writer too?" "He was. He'd spend the morning ploughing the fields, come back home to fill his belly with rice, and fall asleep. In the afternoon, he rested in the yard and spun poems in his head. At the time of the harvest, he anointed the poems with the scent of raw paddy. Those were the real poems – the poetry of Poet Purnachandra." Selim asked, "But Poet, who is Ream?" The poet laughed out loud, "Twenty-four quires make a ream. I need paper to preserve my poems. My grandfather, Poet Purna, couldn't leave any poems behind. Thousands of poems were strewn around in the gardens of the rich – Poet Purna culled many a poem from there.

Actually, humans have nothing – whatever is there, belongs to the birds. Birds are the ones that write poetry and sing their lyrics in unison. For instance, I don't write – Poet Purna compels me to transcribe. Sh... sh... sh... sh... "Where did I get it, or where did Lilabati get it? From the birds... Whatever arose with the hoots of barn owls on a full-moon night in Poet Purnachandra's heart... I got that... from me to Lilabati... and Lilabati reverted it back to me... the hoot of a moon-tinted barn owl... if you hear it, you'd know... shh." Purna used to wake up early morning – before the birds were up. He waited to chant lyrics in chorus with the birds... It was his morning prayers. Some nights, the poet went out to drink in the moonlight. He knew that poems written by the light of the moon survived eternally. He failed in that. Lilabati's shadow obscured his notebook. She gave without asking for anything in return.

The poet couldn't give... Lilabati bestowed on the poet. One moonlit night, the poet started off alone for the port of Tamralipta. Skirting Bargabhima temple, he reached Selim's house and from under his window cried out, "koob, koob, koob," as though the Kubo bird had mistaken the gleaming night for day and was calling out to his companion. Selim woke up and found him. It was midnight for a torpid world. Selim went out and brought the poet in by his hand. "Do you want something to eat, dada[iv]?" "No one needs anything else after a drink of moon rays, Selim. Give me a glass of water." The poet gulped down the water and seemed peaceful. "One feels thirsty after a fill of moonlight. There's only sunshine – like all poems belong to birds and Lilabati." "Is Lilabati a bird?" Selim asked. "I believe so – but I don't know. I forget. Maybe Lilabati is a bird, maybe she isn't." Only the poet understood what he spoke about. He laid down by Selim and slept and called out like a bird in his sleep. The noises he made could only be bird-chirps. Selim kept waking up to check on the poet. The poet stirred at dawn and began to read to Selim the poems Lilabati had sent him. They were various birdcalls. Words. Words are poetry. Selim was spellbound. A spate of moon rays swept the room; then, the midday sun shone clamorously. At times, bird-peeps filled the space. Lots of birds lived inside the poet. The poet met others in the household and said that Selim is his farming partner. Both of them cultivate poetry and chilis in Gurguri island. They grow grapes.

Their chilis are so fiery that they can't sell a single one, and they have to hand out the grapes for free. The birds on the island love grapes. They have to throw the chilis up in the air in the dark of night. That's the reason the stars are piquant. Uncle said, "It would be better to farm watermelons." The poet replied, "I'll give you two hundred acres, please go and farm on the island. Remember, the island often goes walkabouts. Makes it hard to catch.

Suppose it drifts to Portugal with your watermelons? You will have to sell the fruits there, but you can't use your Portuguese earnings here – it'll be a total loss. Chilis are a safer bet." Uncle said, "Sell off the island – otherwise it'll get mislaid someday." "The island is an inheritance from my grandfather, Poet Purnachandra. It'll be a sin to hawk it – I'll end up with a disease. "The island is our ancestral property, I can't sell it. The legal papers of possession were swept away in the deluge the other day. Grandpa' said, 'Good, let them go. No one will be able to sell off the land anymore. This land is ours. It's wicked to sell it. It's immoral to trade off the ancient trees. People should live in their villages and markets. They should farm and keep shops – if they leave, they'll be lost." The poet enjoyed Selim's home. He said that he'll surely light an evening lamp under the holy basil in his yard during the Maghrib Azan. And they must call out Azan when he lights the lamp. The Azan sounds like the blowing of the conch shell to him. They also must believe that the sound of the conch is the call of Azan. The poet left after advising Selim to care for the cattle, farm mindfully, and water plants during the hot months – only then he'll be able to write good poetry. Only then Lilabati will bequeath her poems and won't ask for anything in return. Lalbazar had confiscated the poet's notebook. Its pages had Lilabati's writings. This was his one regret – the notebook was lost.

Avijit reassured him that he will search for it. He did, but to no avail. Selim had approached the Commissioner of Police. They hunted for it in their storeroom – it wasn't there. That was 45 years ago. The Commissioner said that this has been a terribly unjust act – he'd personally go to the poet and seek his forgiveness. When the poet heard this, he said that he's terrified of the police. In America, they choked a man and killed all the Gurguri birds inside him. The birds had tried to get away but could not. In India, a poet has been imprisoned for a long time. Selim asked, "What if the Police Commissioner comes to beg your pardon...? "I'll tell him, 'I want to free the poet who has been jailed'..." Peculiar sounds poured out of the poet's mouth. Selim had come to him with a petition demanding liberty for all poets, writers, and social activists. The poet said, "Human voice doesn't function anymore, Selim. It can't conceive poetry – so, it can't demand freedom. We need bird-calls." From then on, the poet began to protest using his bird voice – at dusk, at the time of Azan, and when conch shells resonate. The night birds fly carrying the poet's words to faraway lands. Their message is simple – F R E E D O M – let the poets breathe. Else, all of us will lose our voices.

----

[i] Lalbazar is the police headquarters of West Bengal.
[ii] 'Di' or 'didi' is an honorific denoting elder sister in Bengali.
[iii] 'Emergency Period' in India refers to the 21 months (1975-1977), when then Prime Minister Indira Gandhi had declared a state of emergency and suspended all human and state rights.
[iv] 'Dada' denotes elder brother in Bengali.

(Translated from the Bengali by Shamita Das Dasgupta, Published in 'The Antonym', February'21)

Nest of a Baya

Are you in touch with anyone from writer Nikhil Datta's family, sir? This is Tridib speaking. Samir felt surprised to hear Tridib's question about Nikhil Datta. Tridib is a junior artist in a theatre group. He keeps busy with acting only. Samiran was not aware of his interest in literature. His theatre group enacted one of Samiran's stories. Since then, they were in touch. Samiran is an author who writes short stories and novels. He's renowned. Publishers spend hours at his house hoping to convince him to publish his book from their publishing houses. He gets invitations to speak in seminars also. His stories have been included in university syllabus. Tridib knew that in his youth, Samiran was well-acquainted with Nikhil Datta. That is why he asked Samiran for help.

Samiran said, all of a sudden, you're asking for Nikhil da?

We've prepared a script from his story 'Babuibasa'. It will be our next production. So, we need consent.

Samiran said, he's not alive.

Tridib said, I know that. But we cannot go on presenting a theatre show without a consent from his family. Where did he live?

Samiran said he lived on Northern Avenue in Paikpara, opposite to a shop named Bengal Sweets. Anyone will show you.

How do I reach there?

Samiran said, take a Uber. Write Paikpara Northern Avenue while stating your location. Once you reach there, ask for Bengal Sweets. Nikhil da's house was surrounded with a beautiful garden. In winter, we used to sit with the sun on our back, in his balcony we've spent so much time.

Will you come with me, sir?

Me! Why me? Samiran feels perplexed.

Meeting writers makes me nervous. Once I visited Dipita Debi to invite her to inaugurate our theatre festival. She started to ask me which of her novels had I read. She also asked me about Tarashankar, Bibhutibhusan and the like. Please come with me, sir.

Samiran said, don't feel scared. He's passed away fifteen years ago.

Still, everyone in a writers family – his wife, son, daughter knows far better than us. Once I went to meet Rajmohan Bandyopadhyay's family to seek permission from them. His daughter started to interrogate us so much! At first she said that she wouldn't give consent without reading the script, and then asked me about my interpretation of the story. When I told her, her comment was that I didn't understand anything. My brain couldn't fathom that topic. Can you imagine, how humiliating it was! She refused to give consent without reading the script.

Samiran said Rajmohan was an extremely proud man, who thought, that he was the best among his contemporary writers. He thought that Graham Greene, Saul Bellow and his peers are nothing compared to his talent. He considered himself worthy of the Nobel award. His daughters are also like him.

Tridib said, I don't feel confident to meet his family alone. I haven't read that much. Although I have different experience with you. It is me only who went to ask for your consent.

Did I try to find out how much you knew?

Tridib said, no sir, rather you gifted me a book. You signed it with my wife Monika's and my name. we preserve it so carefully. We've shown it to so many people and told them how much you love me!

Writer Samiran Basu asks, do people read what I write?

How could you have doubt about that! You have a huge readership. Our Chandana ma'am – renowned actress Chandana Sarkar is spellbound by your stories! She has requested me ample times to take her to your house, at least once, so that she can ask you – how do your stories resemble with her life to such a great extent?

Samiran feels good. He has experienced success now. He is now a wanted writer. Editors wait at his place for hours and hours to publish his writings in the Festival issue of their magazines. They are even ready to republish his old stories. He never thought that he would ever be able to achieve this status. He had to calculate a lot to achieve this place. Getting to know some editors and writers very closely, alienating himself from some of them. Nikhil Datta is not there anymore. But he was an immensely well-respected writer, enormously powerful. He led the editorial board of a leading magazine – in charge of the short story selection process. Samiran remembered that he had submitted his stories to Nikhil Datta ample times. He was the king in his department. Samiran was only twenty or twenty-one years old. Someone said that becoming a close acquaintance of Nikhil Datta would push him towards success very fast. Young writers used to be with him all the time. Nikhil liked them heartily. Those young writers were thirty years or more aged. Nikhil led a movement with them to change the style and form of short stories. He was the centre of rumours. His attires were extremely aristocratic – whether it were a set of shirt-pant, winter suit, or sweaters. Even dhoti-panjabi used to be of very rich fabric. Nikhil had a very fancy choice in everything. He was a talented singer – especially, he sang the songs of Tagore beautifully. However, Samiran's initial experience was not very good.

He used to submit stories, one after another, they were rejected. Nikhil used to tell everyone to keep a copy of the story the intended to submit. At that time, photocopier machine was not available in the market. Xerox Company introduced it to the market. People used carbon copy in those days. Now, hard, printed copies are not required anymore. Writers mail soft copies of their stories, and those do not get lost. Samiran does not use fountain pen now. He works in laptop, even when he goes out of station. Submissions used to get lost from Nikhil Datta's editorial office. He had lost at least three stories submitted by Samiran. It was said that Nikil Datta used to read only a few lines or a paragraph to decide to throw it away. He had indeed decided to select Samiran's fourth story and wrote a letter asking Samiran to meet him. How excited he was after he had received that letter! Nikhil Datta wrote that postcard himself. Samiran met him with an anxious anticipation. Nikhil told him to make a few changes in his story. He also said that rewriting it will make the story much better. Samiran followed his instruction word by word. That story brought him fame. And he became one among Nikhil Datta's closest acquaintances. At that time, being a part of Nikhil Datta's close circle was a boost to become a writer. But Samiran realised that he had miles to go. He would have to write a novel, find a publisher for it. Gradually, he moved away from Nikhil Datta's circle, but kept in touch.

Tridib asks, Sir, will you accompany me to Nikhil Datta's house? Unmindfully, Samiran said, yes, I will. I've never been to his house after his demise. I met Shanta Boudi once in a program celebrating his birthday. It was probably right after the next year of his death. But after that I don't know anything. Maybe the birthday was celebrated again in a program where he was not invited.

But, in that case, he would have at least noticed a piece of news about it. Wouldn't he have known had there been held a party to celebrate his birthday? Who would have celebrated his birthday anyway? Would it be his family?

His son was an ordinary commerce graduate. His daughter however, was a literature student. Nandini was a slim brown-skinned girl. Curly hair and deer eyes. She had deep knowledge of literature. It was her who told Samiran about One Hundred Years of Solitude and Gabriel García Márquez. It was probably 1985. People said that Nikhil Datta asked for Nandini's opinion after she gave the first read to the stories submitted to him. Nandini was a professor. She died suddenly of a cardiac arrest. Her death was extremely agonising. While climbing the stairs of New Delhi flyover, she suddenly pressed her chest tightly and dropped on her knees. She breathed her last in front of Nikhil da while gasping for breath. It took him a long time to absorb that death. He wrote a few stories one after another which reflected his consciousness of death. One of those stories was influenced by The Seventh Seal directed by Ingmar Bergman. Instead of playing chess, the protagonist of that story tried to prevent the death of his daughter while swimming alongside death. And he stopped death. That story brought much fame in his last days. It reminded everyone of The Seventh Seal. Nikhil Datta told him, "my daughter breathed her last right in front of me, my first child, I could as if witness death Samiran, there was nothing I could do, how cruel it looked, it took her away, it took everything away..." Samiran was reminiscing about Nikhil Datta after quite a long time. Nikhil Datta's collection of books was pretty enviable. On the 1500 square feet ground floor of a two-storied house, there was only one living room. The rest of the place was full with books. Wall to wall shelves were full with books. A librarian, who was fond of Nikhil Datta had organized the books – an archive of classics, translation of Indian and foreign writers, and books originally written in English. Nikhil played the role of his teacher. He used to tell him which books to read and lend him books from his own collection. A writer should focus on both – reading and writing. Samiran decided to visit Nikhil Datta's house. He was craving for that library – books in every room, fiction, novels, articles, translation, Indian, foreign...all great books. Even his book also found a place there.

Tridib said that he would bring a car after two days, on Sunday and accompany Samiran to Nikhil Datta's house. Tridib came.

Samiran lives in Garia. Via Eastern Metropolitan Bypass, it takes a long time to reach from north to south, Garia to Pikepara. Bidhan Nagar Road station, a road alongside the canal, Belgachhia railway-bridge, water reserve on the left side of the road, Tala Park...everything has changed. Huge advertising hoardings on the E.M. Bypass and colourful smiles have changed the face of the city. Multistoried complexes have been developed far away in the outskirts of the city. Huge office buildings and shopping malls have been built on both sides of the road. And then, Dhapa. It's not a mount, but wastes. All the garbage of Kolkata have accumulated in Dhapa and turned it into a mounted hill. Samiran has not been to this side for a long time. He does not go out much. Either he mails his stories or people from magazines or newspapers come and meet at his place to collect his submission.

Samiran couldn't identify anything in this highway. Where does he visit except meetings or programs? Traveling only. Madhupur, Jashidi, Hazaribag, Gopalpur, Chilka lake, Ajanta, and Ellora. Sometimes he visits abroad as well. Last year, he visited the United States. Both sides of Virginia was covered with snow even at the end of March. All the trees were blank. How solitary was that road! We can never experience that kind of solitude.

130 crore people have congested the roads, streets, forests and even jungles. Nikhil Datta's house was very beautiful. It had a flower garden on the front yard. And, the backyard had Kerala coconut trees, guava, mango etc. He used to see Nikhil Datta on his front lawn reading books while lying down half on his deck chair. One day he saw him reading Samiran's first published collection of short stories, 'Math Bhange Kaalpurush.' Samiran could recognise the cover even from a distance. It was the most

beautiful moment in his young life. Samiran didn't move. After finishing one story Nikhil Datta looked up. In his usual ethnic dress, Nikhil Datta seemed very close to his heart that day. Who reads a young writer's book! And now, he does not have even one single copy of that book - his first book. Samiran could not remember Northern Avenue, Bengal Sweets, Tala Water Reserve – everything very clearly. The double-storied house at the end of the road – facing the sweet shop. Where is it? Samiran got down from the car and went to Bengal Sweets. He wanted to buy sweets for boudi. How old is she now? Seventy-five maybe.

She was twelve years junior than Nikhil Datta. Nikhil da would have become 87 or 88 years old by now. An age of a time has passed. A huge house is standing there. The name of that house was Babuibasa. Babui was the name of his youngest child – a son. Is that the same house or is he mistaken? He asked at the sweet shop about Nikhil Datta's house and they responded back asking how he was related. Well he was not related – he was here only to meet the family of a writer. Samiran introduced himself and the employee said, you're also a writer, Sir, I've seen you on TV on several occasions. And then slightly surprised, he said, they don't live here anymore, Sir. Look at that eight-storied building, on the same land. It was a promoting project. What! Samiran cried out instantly. Babuibasa has been demolished-? Yes sir, the deal was of 3 crore rupees.

After five years of the writer's death, everyone left. Tridib asked, where have they moved? Is an address available? I don't know anything about that. Lot of houses are being demolished, everyone is shifting with their luggage by lorry. I have been living in Pikepara only. There is almost no old house left here – it's the storm of development. Nothing more was left to say. Samiran considers going in front of the multistoried building. That house, its garden, the library of that house – Samiran was feeling very sad. It would have been better if he had not come. Tridib asked, what should we do, Sir? Samiran didn't respond to any questions on his way back. It took him a long time to cross the Eastern Bypass – submerged in darkness and glowing with light. Traffic jam and countless people all around. Among these people Nikhil Datta's family, Shanta boudi and Babui are also lost. Are they lost? They've left in exchange for 3 crore rupees.

They've taken all those books, the horses and elephants of Panchmuda. Shanta boudi was an avid reader. Babui was not that much of a speaker. Samiran gifted a pair of horses crafted by the artisans of Panchmuda to Babui in his reception. The arrangement was huge! The entire street in front of that house was decorated with a pandal. The house was a dead end on that street and that's why that kind of decoration was possible. After reaching Garia, Samiran told Tridib, go to Ajanta Publishers in College Street and ask them about the address. They have published all his books. Tridib again called after a few days. 'I've found out their whereabouts. His son stays at an apartment in Newtown Co-operative. You'll accompany me, won't you, sir? Meeting a writer's family alone feels strange! New town is further ahead after Salt Lake. It's a new township. Government has provided land to several cooperatives at a cheaper rate.

All the houses are multistoried. This new township is not as populated as Garia, Pikepara or other areas of proper Kolkata. It's an organized township and the plan is very beautiful. The housing cooperative they wanted was huge and they had to really search for Block F. it's a Sunday afternoon. Tridib had an appointment for today only. He got the phone number from Nikhil Datta's publisher. In a solitary afternoon, they used the elevator to reach the seventh floor. The nameplate of the apartment read, 'Babui basa.' Samiran felt a faster heartbeat. He can still feel goose-bumps when he visualises Nikhil Datta reading his first short story collection, 'Math Bhange Kaalpurush.' Tridib pushes the doorbell. Samiran felt Nikhil Datta wearing his ethnic dress would open the door. Samiran, is it really you? We haven't met for such a long time, Samiran. You've become famous now, is everyone forgetting me, Samiran? Haven't I written anything significant, Samiran! Nikhil has shifted here after his death. Samiran planned to collect the copy of his first book from Babui. He would like to keep it. The first book is like the first child. Nikhil Datta was unable to write anything at all after he had lost his first child. The person who opened the door indeed looked like Nikhil Datta. Babui, in his mature age, completely resembles his father.

Wearing pant and casual shirt, and expensive specs on his eyes Babui invited them in. Samiran said, I used to visit your Pikepara house very frequently. Can you recognise me? Babui smiles, yes, I can recognise you. Please sit down. Are you an actor too? Samiran got stunned. He visibly looked pale. Babui didn't even recognise him. Before he could correct Babui, Tridib introduced him. Babui said apologetically, yes, it's really very old stuff, I made a mistake, I'm sorry. What about your mother? Mother also passed away four years after father's demise. After that only we moved here. Ma didn't want to leave that house. What would you like, coffee or tea? Tridib brought out the consent form and a cheque of Rs. 10,000. Babui's wife came in. Babui introduced her.

They have a single child – who stays at a residential convent school in Darjeeling. They visit him once a year and he also comes home once – during the summer vacation. And Babui manages income tax, GST, and other accounting related works from home. His wife Gopa is a teacher at a convent school. They've seen the consent. Sipping the coffee Samiran asked, do you still have those large horses of Panchmura which I gifted during your wedding? Babui smiles again, we couldn't bring everything during the shifting of the house. I came to take the copy of my first book which was kept in your library. Because, I don't have any copy of it. Where are those books – Nikhil da's magnificent collection? Babui said, we couldn't bring those. We brought only some of the furniture. We left everything else there and the promoter took care of it. All the books! Yes. Babui's wife said, where would we have kept those in our 1100 square-feet apartment? Samiran didn't wait anymore. Babui abandoned his archive while moving to a new house. Samiran's first book was also among one of those abandoned ones.

Tridib and he returned through EM Bypass. Samiran was whispering, "Nikhil da lost. He was defeated. You went out of breath while swimming against death, Nikhil da." Through the vast darkness on the right side of EM Bypass is located the garbage field, Dhapa. All the garbage of Kolkata have accumulated there and formed a huge mount. That mount caught fire in the dark. Discarded things are destroyed in Dhapa's fire. Books, crafted horses of Panchmura. One day a promoter came here to discard 3 trucks of abandoned books and set fire to those before going back. Those books were burning in a temperature of 451 degrees. It was Nikhil Datta who made him read Ray Bradbury.

Samiran's first book 'Math Bhange Kaalpurush' was burning too. The books were destroyed to demolish the old house and build a new multistoried building which would not have a single book on any floor of it. That same fire could be seen faraway, on that mounted garbage. Samiran felt the heat of his burning book. While uttering the name of his first book, he was crossing the burning mount. He kept crossing. And the mount with those burning books, kept moving along with him.

(Translated from the Bengali by Dolonchampa
Chakraborty)

Two   Women

They were supposed to descend at an encampment township.The kind of muffin appeals to the most common Indian habitat something between half rural and half urban consisting shops, marketplaces, police station, watch house, offices, sub offices and lots of people with work or without. One between them has come from Ballavpur, Ranigunj crossing the river Damodar while the other from a village,existing somewhere on the rest bank of the great river. They are two, Sundori Dasi and Annadarani, two crone, one is overage and the other recently aged.

Annadarani, the newly gray one, has husband in her home but merely as a surviving one lying in bed. She had a son also but never returned after leaving in search of livelihood so far. Her husband is now a decrepit but as he once rescued her, gave her doll's house so always at the back of her mind, she carries a sense of gratitude towards him and it would be unjust to declare that she is devoid of every trace of love for him also.

Her man is now nothing but a bundle of flesh like element left in the corner of a room. It's her sole responsibility to feed him. Think about the name, Annadarani, the goddess of paddy fields on earth. How can she allow her own household to continue without rice?

Very old Sundori Dasi is in barren white stuff now, mostly unclean, tattered and overstitched.

Husband passed away at dawn of her life, diseased son has expired also at the dusk, leaving behind him three kids and young wife. Both of them were coming from Mejia to reach Naopahari but in the trans of dozing, none could notice when the bus touched this Motukboni in the lap of hill, receding from Na'pahari eight miles back. It was the conductor who made the two without fare climbing down the stairs. None of them was acquainted with Na'pahari before but even within dozing, Annadarani's intuition gifted her doubts. She is clad in a scarlet cotton with red and white plastic bangles in hand.

Comparing to the other, she holds more strength, therefore, knocked Sundoridasi....

"Hey..oldie..wake up..seems it has come.."

Half asleep, oldie, Sundoridasi uttered.... "Gosh..so fiery it is today." She was closing her eyelids with the blazing world outside then, peeping through the open door. True it is. Too much sunny a day. Even the numb lap of the valley is overflowing with the rays like the body of a mirror, like the bosom of a river with glittering sands. And winds, similar to the heatwave of a huge furnace belonging to occasions, enough to steam the whole frame. Memories of her own marriage, smell of mutton curry, like occasional flashes of lightning, were emerging in Annadarani's drowsy mind. A bowl of hot rice dabbed in mutton gravy tastes no less than ripe tartar slightest remembrance of which makes mouth watery.

It seems as if she has eaten only once in her lifetime. The shadow has turned hazy, sunburnt. Within room, a bundle of flesh like element namely husband and under the sky, blaze. She feels an unending burning within. She fails to remember who got married once or if there was any feast in the world ever. They were seated, crouched, at the farthest end of their bus, over dusts of numerous feet of the passengers. As the shutters were down, a peculiar half lit cloud hovered within it. Their dozing and nap were shattered by the shouts of the conductor long after. The bus vanished in the highway towards Purulia. They were left behind, by the side of Motukboni hill. It was Sundoridasi who was first recognized.

"it's not Na'pahari..Look.."

"Hm.."

Annadarani is worried, much worried now.

"I'm insane.. If I try to do one thing, it turns into another..What was you doing dear married? Done with sense also?" Annadarani didn't answer.

None of them could stand the scorching sunshine. Sundoridasi had started facing the typical irritation of skin full of prickly. They allowed themselves to be seated in the shadow of a huge Akashmoni, over dusts again with their legs stretched. Unlike the townships, the area was absolutely devoid of offices, marketplaces and most importantly, the public. They had turned utter astonished.

In front of them,hill,behind them,hill.In fact,where they were standing, perhaps a portion of the plain between two hills.

"Is it the house of death? O married.."

Slight mutterings are heard from Sundoridasi. Just aged Annada was then scratching her head for lice, wearing scarlet cotton with red-white plastic bangles. The cotton had slipped from her head. It was on her shoulders.

"Why did the bloody conductor leave us here? let death devour him..bloody.." Heat has made the lice of her head too much restless. Annadarani desperately scratches her hair with fingers. She had tied her non sticky, untidy lot by a thin string. Within a second she makes them loose to fly in the air. As they were bereft of oil long since, urge to flee instantly beyond the circle like dead leaves. "Now what?"

Whispers the all white one. "No way." The track seems a grim, burnt black snake, deadly silent. With a narrow turn, it has disappeared to the north touching southward, destined to Purulia. The village seems not very vast with very few huts, dry fields, empty crops by the side of hills. Nobody is seen anywhere in the serene sunny noon.A half open shed of beetle leaves and cigarettes is taking midday nap in the bus stand. And a hump backed aged with half closed eyes and swollen legs is seen seated within a tea-shop.The kettle is smeared with deep carbon stamps.

The fire is put out. Everything appears fast asleep here and there. They observe the whole scene with minute details which makes them depressed bit by bit. Finally, relieved, they start waiting under the Akashmoni, fixed. This is a place from where the even the idea of arranging food or clothing is ridiculous. They have realised already.

Even if they beg, nobody is capable of giving alms, certain. They consider the village as another beggar's den. "What's the time now?" Enquires Sundori Dasi. Watching the sky, Annada replies.. "Twelve perhaps.. The sun is above our heads."

"Sure? So much?"

"No doubt" Annadarani replies in negative. Again the white one feels an acute sense of relief. A pure indifference surges her eyes and the whole frame. Repeating the age old habit, She drops the cover of her breast. But before that, makes a quick survey with restless pupils if anybody there. The manner of dropping her breast cover is too ancient, she knows by herself. Still, the feel of a throbbing every time she does that in open space never ceases. The whole body is moist in perspiration. The sun, the sweat and the heat - all have mingled to make an old lying, dusted. That particular kind of heat is a devil. It arouses only the urge of lying down and then, inevitably, sleep. The white one again mutters.. "Oye..how much passed after twelve?" Again Annadarani in scarlet watches the sky.. "Half past twelve I think.." "What does it mean? "Thirty minutes have gone after twelve and more thirty is needed to strike one" "Why so?" Sundoridasi tries to get the meaning, fanning her bosom.

"Sixty minutes make an hour"

"Who said so?"

Annadarani turns standstill to face the asking. For a while, stops killing lice. Failing to find enough smartness to answer, she feels somewhat ashamed. A blush appears in her brownish face. Then lowering her forehead, she whispers..

"The man."

"Who?"

"Don't you know?"

Sundoridasi smiles,baring toothless gum. "Oh! I forgot. Your man has not yet fled to the pyre." Annadarani feels electrified, trembling within. The widow doesn't know he is almost near the pyre. Practically, he is on the verge of collapsing permanently. The only capacity remains to touch the dilapidated veranda from room, crawling. Eyes have lost all the language, the memory, next to nil. She is wearing this scarlet cotton and red white bangles only because he still breathes.

"Enjoy much na? Huh.." Asks Sundoridasi.

"Enjoy.." Annadarani nodes looking at the other side. Obvious enjoyment really. Suddenly she becomes pale and tries to hide her face with palms.

"What does an aged bed fellow do at old age? Oye proudest..Tell na? "If you had your own,would realize" Replies Annadarani, hissing.

It doesn't become clear whether Sundori Dasi hears it or not, maybe she is overhearing everything and pretending to be unheard, staring at Motukboni hill. Sometimes, hills camouflage folk as clouds.

Oh...the stony land hasn't drenched in rain for ages. The two had become acquainted by faces in the morning at the ferry of Mejia. Mejia of Bankura district situated at one bank of Damodar where on the other carries Ballavpur of Ranigunj under district of Burdwan. Sundoridasi was coming from the opposite, crossing the river. Annadarani was going in her left direction, to Ranigunj railway station. They met in between as now-a-days the river bed is stark dry, giving abundance for the whole to cross by walking. First one had crossed half of the bay while the second one

the rest of it. Annadarani in scarlet cotton had enquired..
"I wanna go Andal...Has the train departed or yet to arrive?"

Sundori Dasi in all white stuff had replied in the negative, informing..

"Next one is after two hours..Oi..Where is the ghat? How distant is Mejia hence? Standing at mid river, the married one replied.. "From the mooring..One mile..But has the train really departed?"

"If you doubt..Go and verify.."

Then Annadarani stopped proceeding further. She began to return. Return seemed inevitable as the train scheduled after two long hours. She didn't know exactly why she was aiming at Andal but she knew she had to go somewhere. The thought drove her out of the house. Who would feed her if she remained relaxing within? But she must have had to feed her man so left her damp comfort zone. She was seated under a great Banyan with palm on her cheeks after a round at the wharf. If she could leave two hours before, she would have been at Andal. May the place accommodate her food or clothing. May the place bring a solution. Definitely it would and that's why the train departed before she caught it. The white one also had walked along her, even sat muted by the side. Before them was the blank river only then and above, a whirlwind of dry sand. Sundoridasi had touched her shoulder..

"Why Andal? Where's the home?"

Depressed Annadarani had turned towards her, startled. She had whispered, watching head to toe of the olden.

"To manage livelihood"

"Anybody know? There?"

"Nope.." Like a falling leaf, Annadarani had waved her head. She had suppressed the tears which were desperate to flow. known..Who is known to her in the world? It's been a long anybody has asked for her whereabouts.

Parents have passed away many years ago. Both of her two brothers had gone for work in Chinakuri coal mine, selling land and hut, everything but never returned. The white one had commented.. "No work on the other bank.. How will you manage? Ballavpur paper mill is lock out..

All of the three factories of Andal are closed..Who will give you money? Where to go?" Almost broken, the married one had wailed..

"Then..What to do?" The widow was silent. She stretched her eyes over the river. In this time of draught, the river dresses up like another widow with no color, perhaps without a soul also. In the next turn, Annadarani had enquired..

"What about your destination? "Here..In this bank..To the village..Mejia."

"Whose house? Relative?"

"Not really.." The widow had declared..

"To earn.."

"Where is rice or saree? Look at me.."

"Why? No family here? Nobody to donate to a widow in starvation, something? Anything? "

All starved widows are facing drought here..Rain hasn't visited for many years..All are in fasting now..Who will help you?"

"Then..Where to go?" As if both of them had uttered in the same breath..Where to go? One silently and the other, in words. Married Annadarani had withdrawn her eyes from the widow as the latter had concentrated on the crimson parting of her hair. Finally, it had shifted it's centre also after a period. They decided to discuss. One was going to Andal while the other was coming for Mejia. But nobody completed their journey to their respective destinies. None went to Andal or anyone to Mejia. Like beggars, they boarded the bus from the reed, took seats over dust in a corner. The conductor was too humane. He allotted full concessions to their fares when they clutched his feet.

But they couldn't reach Na'pahari township where they decided to reach after discussion. Instead,they arrived at this hilly Motukboni. They had started gathering each other's secrets as much as possible since the river. Without taking her eyes off from the stark sun, Annadarani tries to hurt Sundoridasi.. "Hello ! Then you are living with two husbands.." Sucking dry lips with drier tongue,she utters again.. "You are a success to help two to pyre." A nameless shadow grasps the copper face of Sundoridasi within a moment. As the shadow surpasses, her eyes blink. She tosses her head violently, loudly breathes through moist bosom in perspiration as if igniting a dying furnace,like prodding a lowering flame. "How many mouths to feed? Annadarani again pricks.

Killing a lice by nails,the widow points at her five fingers. "Daughter in law devours the son?" "Notice me..I have eaten my son.." Replies Sundoridasi, hissing.

Annadarani brushes knife of her tongue more aptly this time.. "When did you swallow your man?" The widow moved her face away..

"Long ago..Within youth.."

"Then why again?" Annadarani swirls her wrist exactly like the hood of a fierce snake before Sundoridasi.The red and white plastic sparkles. Olden Sundoridasi can't make her eyes estranged from them. Her blood warms within, eyes start itching. She has half fed her members with flakes of wheat anyhow in last two days. And since leaving the house in the morning today, nothing has entered her stomach until noon. In the house, three of her own dearest are surviving, demurred and the witch, the husband eater, and her daughter in law are suffering from high fever. She nails pricklies of her skin forcefully and flickers her tongue as a snake does.

"Oye..what will you do with your enlarged husband?" Annadarani maintains silence. "I had son..Even if he is no more but I have grandchildren still..No one is a corpse.. The paleness of Annadarani rises steadily.

Her eyes become burdened. As Annadarani starts facing the sound of a waterfall made of her own tears within the vapid sunny noon at the stony valley, Sundoridasi, using corner of her thumb, almost like a spade, peels her sweat on the dust. Both of them refuse to see the face of the other for long. And then, the widow proposes..

"Get up"

"Where?"

"To beg" Answers Sundoridasi.

"Stupid" Annadarani smiles.

"Where to beg?"

"Then what?"

Then what..The married one turns fixed watching the sun. It's mid noon. Sixty minutes makes an hour and twenty four hours makes a day. Everything she had learnt from her man once. Now he has lost his own humor, can't identify anyone, fails to remember anything. He only demands to eat every time, sitting within. "It's been a long since rain hasn't arrived na? The widow again parts her lips.. "Yup..Damodar is carrying only sand..Roads are carrying merely sunshine and whirl winds.."

"Does your husband know these facts?" Annadarani gets stunned. Her sunburnt visage becomes more stoned and her heart,more heavy,compared to the tor. The weight seems too grave. It's true. Her husband knows nothing.

It's been many years as if for many decades and ages,clouds haven't shed rains. And all the streets are empty,no work on either bank,no clothing,no food as the cloud hasn't poured. Mankind has been dozing and sleeping like street dogs for time immemorial. All the fields are like her cracked heels. Dirt is flying, dust is entering, walking is increasing pain. Stones are too hot to hold foot. Does his dying husband know all these vast details? Does he know the fire is still alive, which had ignited through the clashing of just dry leaves in the hills of Mejiya some days ago? Does he know his goddess of rice has left his home to beg for rice? Does he know, leaving for Andal, she is now seated beside a widow at the valley of Motukboni? Does he know the widow has neither husband nor son but a house full of grandsons and daughters? Nope. He knows nothing. Within the darkest corner of his room, he only breathes, lying. He keeps no track with the world outside,only use to spread his tongue whenever she touches his lips with any edible element. Annadarani states bluntly.. "No..He has no information.." Suddenly Sundoridasi gets shocked. She has forgotten what she had asked. She just manages to pronounce.. "Who doesn't know?"

Annadarani doesn't reply. Again silence overpowers the two. They continue watching the highway. The bus has gone to Purulia via Madhukunda. When it will return, it's unknown. After some time, Annadarani asks.. "When did the son die?" Sundoridasi's face turns expressionless. She feels an utter blankness within her brain like a field facing drought. She mutters.. "What did you say? In sixty hours..let's calculate.."

"Have you gone insane?" The widow smiles dryly. She can realize now-a-days her brain stops working properly at times. Who can adjust the deaths of husband and son being wholly sane? It might be adjusted though if hope remains with the leftovers. But with which assurance or support? She has neither property nor anything. Three grandchildren, lamps of their forefathers, are biting incessantly. Her daughter in law is shedding tears, mum, dark faced day and night. As if all the liability rests on her, on the quaggy.

Annadarani again asks..

"Food and cloth..Be managed?"

"Who knows?" Sundoridasi waves her head.

"Your case is different..Much better..Grandchildren.." With a shrunken shoulder and bent spine, the widow remains seated as if in another stone. Yes, her case is different but in which way, wish, she could know. She is on the road due to them, to get relief, to sit over dust if something is earned, something, at least one or two rupees, stirring. "Had breakfast? Husband..I mean.."

Annadarani nodes her neck silently, keeping jaws unflinched. How could she break his fast? With which? She had nothing and that fear of nothingness had driven her out of the house. She has grown a fear within even to stand before him recently. Her body quenches,breathing ceases in times of his bouts of hunger. Sundoridasi again asks.. "Where to find water here?"

"Somewhere.." Mutters Annadarani.

"I have some parched rice.."

"Really? Where? Within your pouch?" Annadarani turns restless.

"Wait..The eldest among grandsons had tied while leaving.."

"Happy family" Annadarani whispers. Happy family. The widow grimly smiles with toothless gum. She had to leave hiding the grains. If the venomous devils could see, would swallow instantly, snatching. Annadarani declares..

"I have two rupees"

"Rupees?" Sundoridasi gets amazed with the news.

"Yup..The man had tied at the end of my saree while leaving.." Annadarani mutters.

"Oh! Such a sweet household and husband..Though old but never forgets to take such care." Annadarani listens, silent. Her face is dark. What a happy household. These two rupees were her last refuge. If she had left the money,he would devour it before dusk breaks. She peers fixedly at the widow Sundoridasi, thinking about her merry house ,full of grandchildren. Sundoridasi is viewing her also. Both of them doze, keeping eyes on one another. Meanwhile, the sun prepares to voyage on another half. But in reality, the span of a day is like a hill itself in this area. For the demise, it needs much much more. Dozing, Sundori Dasi enquires.. "Where is the water to eat the grains?" Annadarani lures..

"Let's go..Find some lake..Need a bath badly..Oh ! I feel so hungry.." "Will you?Really?" The widow's eyes glisten with the lust of an unseen water body. They wake up. Waking, start walking. Leaving the heated pitch highway, they find a dusty track on the left through a bush. One behind another, the married follow the widow along like two pilgrims. They stagger with perspired frames, they trudge, bending, they proceed like drunkards. Soon, crossing some distance, a large pool is discovered. It seems the sun melts some silver in the furnace. The water is twinkling similar to the pupils of the two oldies. Both of them burst crying together.. "Will bathe" Together, they shout aloud and repeat the utterance. They have to wash away all unbearable burns, dust and dirt of the day from their physics in the pool water. They desire to clean the other's wounds even, like sorrow, pang, agony, everything. The widow fantasizes how happy the married is with the geezer and the married imagines how wealthy it feels to have a house full of grandsons and daughters. Sundoridasi suggests not to make the sarees wet. "No need at all..leave them here..Nobody is around.." Then they dive into the sapphire blue water, dive being acutely alert, peeping cautiously as virgins do in their shivering merriment during playtime. They become peacefully sheltered behind the water. Annadarani exclaims..

"Cool.." Sundoridasi plunges deep within water. None of them have drenched their skin with such chill for long. Playing with water, Annadarani tries to get confirmation.. "Certainly..And the rupees? enough to have sweet meats and tea for two? "Sure.." As destined, gradually the time arrives at last when they have to leave the water. With sunken naked structures similar to ancient ruined shrines, two women emerge above water. As soon as their feet touch the ground, both turn alarmed all of a sudden. As if a soft sound is heard, as if someone is coming, as if dry leaves are being crunched under unknown treading. Conscious enough, the two women start running to pounce on their desolate sarees. Wonder..Nobody had come..It was the wind of a departing day..The trees were awakening from the slumber of noon, the slumber of sun, the slumber of lethargy, the slumber of surviving from fire..And the sound was overflowing the whole valley.. Realizing, Sundori Dasi bursts out in laughter.. "What? What happened? Annada? Look.." Annadarani looks at herself, astonished..

"Really..what happened!" Their sarees have been exchanged by their owners. Sundori Dasi is clad in scarlet cotton now and Annadarani's body is carrying the white stuff. They are standing silently, shivering. How does it happen? Automatically? Or is it the reflection of their super egos? Had they wished this? They start their journey again towards the highway, together. The time all the light was dying on earth..The hill was overshadowing the whole universe.

(Translated from the Bengali by Sonali Chakraborty)